G.I.JOE
THE RISE OF COBRA

MOVIE NOVELIZATION

adapted by Brian James
based on the story by Michael Gordon and
Stuart Beattie & Stephen Sommers
and the screenplay by Stuart Beattie and
David Elliot & Paul Lovett

Simon Spotlight
New York   London   Toronto   Sydney

Based on Hasbro's G.I. JOE® Characters

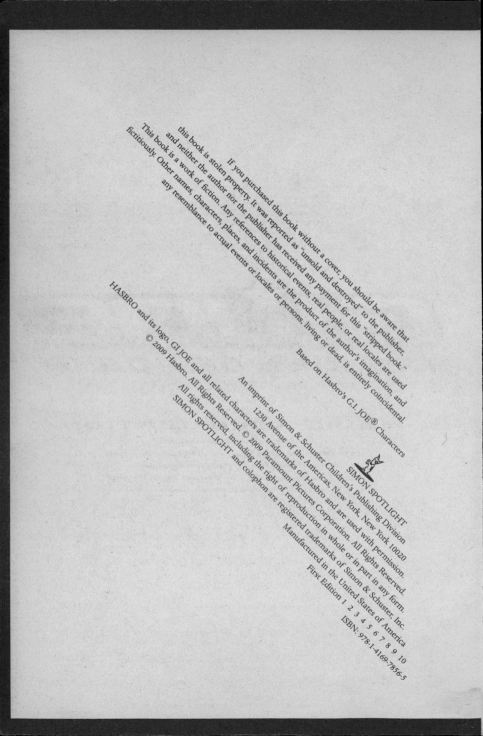

SIMON SPOTLIGHT

An imprint of Simon & Schuster Children's Publishing Division
1230 Avenue of the Americas, New York, New York 10020

Manufactured in the United States of America
First Edition 1 2 3 4 5 6 7 8 9 10
ISBN: 978-1-4169-7856-5

prologue

Paris, 1641

The imposing prison towers rose high above the streets and disappeared into the heavy night fog. A battalion of guards was stationed on the street and another on the parapets above to protect the intimidating fortress known as Bastille. The most dangerous criminals in the kingdom of France were held there. The guards kept a tight grip on their long pikes, ready to stop anyone from escaping. In 1641, France was at war, and the criminals were more than just thieves—they were enemies.

The most treacherous enemies were kept deep inside the prison. The narrow halls were barely lit with the flicker of torches, and the moans of starving prisoners could be heard everywhere. As two guards made their way through the corridor, they took no notice of the whimpering captives. Their orders were clear. They were only concerned with one prisoner: James McCullen.

"On your feet, you Scottish pig!" one of the guards shouted into McCullen's cell. The rats scurried out of the way, but McCullen didn't budge. He glared through the bars at the two guards. The torchlight reflected off the red square medallion around his neck and made McCullen's eyes appear to glow as he defied the guard's command. Then a mean smile split across his face. "Going for a wee walk, are we?" he asked.

The guards weren't in the mood for his attitude. They unlocked the cell door and barged in. It took all of their combined strength to lift McCullen and drag him to his feet. With his hands and feet chained, McCullen didn't put up much of a struggle as he was led through the dim halls and into the courtyard. He felt the fresh air around him and breathed it in. Even though the air was damp and cold, it tasted good. After days in the disgusting prison, he was enjoying the moment of freedom.

But it didn't last long. Once they crossed the courtyard, the guards led him back inside the thick prison walls. A sudden wave of hot air rushed against McCullen's face as they entered a large room where several prison workers were slaving in front of a blazing furnace. McCullen noticed the red hot chunk of metal they were molding and wondered why he'd been brought there. His eyes continued to take in the scene, darting back and forth across the room as the guards chained him to the wall.

A moment later the warden approached from a shadowy corner, unrolling a scroll he held in his hands. McCullen suddenly realized that he was about to hear his sentence. "James McCullen," the warden read from the scroll, "you have been found guilty of treason for the sale of military arms to the enemies of our lord, King Louis XIII, even whilst you sold arms to our lord himself."

"Your king is a vile bag of filth who murders his own allies!" McCullen shouted. He had no regrets for what he'd done. He'd never been concerned with taking sides in any military conflict. His only concern was making sure he got enough money from whichever side was willing to pay him. As his sentence was being handed down, he realized that he hadn't earned nearly enough from the king this time. "I should've charged him double," he told the warden.

The warden ignored McCullen's outburst and continued reading from the scroll. "You tried to overthrow the Crown in conspiracy with its enemies!"

McCullen lunged forward in a violent rage. "Unlike your simpleton king," he said, sneering, "his enemies know that the McCullen destiny is to *run* the wars, not simply supply arms." Then he flashed an evil grin, knowing that the man who controlled the weapons had the power to control the war. Even if the king had him locked up, McCullen knew he was still the keeper of the power.

The warden raised one eyebrow and stared at the prisoner. Every prisoner brought before him swore revenge. "Do you have anything *else* to say before the sentence is carried out?" he asked.

"Yes, I do," McCullen growled. "Clan McCullen is far bigger and more powerful than any of you could ever imagine. My sons will continue to rise long after I am gone. As will their sons. And, God willing, *their* sons." Another smile crept over his face as the thought of revenge took hold. Then he made his final vow. "It shall not end with my death."

"Oh, we're not going to *kill* you," the warden said. By then he was smiling too. He glanced over at the workers, who were removing a fiery metal object from the furnace. "We're going to make an *example* of you," he continued. Then he gave a nod to the workers, and they walked toward him. As they got closer, McCullen saw the object they were carrying. It was the chunk of metal he had noticed on his way inside. He could now make out that it was actually a mask. He suddenly realized that his punishment would, indeed, be worse than death, and for the first time in his life he was afraid.

The warden glanced back at the scroll still in his hands

and began to read again. "So that no man, woman, nor child may ever see your treacherous face again," he said, "you shall wear this mask for the term of your natural life."

McCullen struggled against his chains, but it was no use. There was nowhere to go. As the red hot mask was brought up to his face, its hinges creaked open and McCullen began to panic. He screamed as the searing metal touched his skin. His screams filled the room and could be heard even on the streets outside the prison. The workers sealed the mask's lock as McCullen continued to fight off the pain with thoughts of revenge.

Then, just before he blacked out, he vowed to make them regret the day they ever tried to bring the McCullen clan down.

Outside NATO's massive headquarters in Brussels, the flags of many countries flapped in the wind. The top generals from each member nation were gathered for an important meeting. Mr. McCullen, the man in charge of MARS (Military Armaments Research Syndicate) Industries, had come to tell the generals about the newest weapon his company had created.

Everyone had been waiting for the completion of this top secret weapon for months. Many believed this new technology might be the key to ending all wars, but some, like Clayton Abernathy, also known as General Hawk, were not so convinced. He knew that new weapons always brought about new conflicts.

A sudden silence filled the room as Mr. McCullen

stood up and asked the military men for their attention. Like his ancestors, McCullen was a fearsome figure. He towered over everyone, and his booming voice easily quieted the room. A red medallion hung around his neck, the very same one worn by the doomed founder of Clan McCullen. In the dimmed light, the red from the heirloom gave McCullen's eyes a faint glow as he began his presentation.

"War used to be the exception," he told the military commanders. "Now it is the new state of play. Tragic as they are to fight, wars must be won." The listeners nodded their heads regrettably. They were too aware of the many conflicts that had flared up across the globe in recent years. NATO had lost a lot of good men and women trying to bring about peaceful solutions, and that was why they hoped MARS Industries had finally come up with something that would help them end these struggles, once and for all. "But perhaps," he continued, "wars don't have to be as destructive as they've been in the past."

A series of blueprint images came to life on the large flat-screen monitor behind him. The people in the room studied the diagrams of tiny mechanical gadgets called nanomites. It was hard for them to believe that these microscopic weapons could be the most dangerous ones ever invented.

"Nanomites are perfect little soldiers," McCullen

explained, "originally developed to isolate and destroy cancer cells. But at MARS Industries we discovered how to program them to do almost anything. For instance," he said, "nanomites can eat metal."

He asked his audience to direct their attention to the screen behind him. In a demonstration of the new weapons' abilities, the two soldiers on-screen faced down a tank. One of them fired a shoulder-launched missile at the vehicle. The missile streaked across the sky and scored a direct hit, but the tank didn't explode. Instead, the warhead burst into a silver cloud made up of millions of nanomites. The mechanical creatures had gone to work in an instant, devouring the tank, like piranhas.

The tank vanished from the screen in a matter of seconds.

"Each warhead contains seven million nanomites that have the ability to eat anything from a single tank to an entire city," McCullen proudly told the generals. On the screen, the nanomites swarmed toward a jeep filled with a camera crew. As the people in the jeep started running for their lives, one of the soldiers hit a kill switch and the nanomites stopped dead in their tracks, inches in front of the jeep. "Once the target has been destroyed, a kill switch short-circuits the nanomites," McCullen said, "preventing any *unwanted* destruction and innocent casualties."

The room erupted into applause. Everyone in the

room agreed that the new weapon was a breakthrough—everyone, that is, except General Hawk.

Hawk narrowed his dark eyes and wrinkled his forehead doubtfully. "Guess you'll be the first arms dealer up for the Nobel Peace Prize," he called out into the now silent auditorium.

A few members chuckled, but most silently awaited McCullen's response. McCullen was a good sport about it. He smiled and replied, "I prefer the term 'armament solutions engineer.'"

Hawk raised an eyebrow and then laughed perfunctorily. Suddenly the tension disappeared and the entire room laughed. McCullen's smile grew wider too. Finally it was time to get down to business, which was why he was there in the first place.

"Gentlemen!" he said excitedly. "I'm pleased to announce that tomorrow morning your first order of nanomite warheads will ship from my factory."

The workers at the MARS Industries factory, hidden deep in the deserts of Kyrgyzstan, were finishing the first warheads as the meeting was taking place.

The meeting came to a close, and McCullen made his way out of the briefing room. General Hawk watched him shake hands with many of the military commanders on their way out. He waited until McCullen was alone, then Hawk gave a nod to his aide, Cover Girl. It was time they made their move.

Hawk was grinning as he approached McCullen. Holding his hand out, he introduced himself. "Mr. McCullen, I'm Clayton Abernathy."

"I know who you are, General Hawk," McCullen said as he shook Hawk's hand. "It's an honor to meet a man of your many accomplishments."

He invited Hawk to walk with him, and the General accepted. Cover Girl followed close behind with Zartan, McCullen's aide, walking beside her. It only took her a second to notice Zartan was copying the way she walked.

"Are you mimicking me?" she asked, annoyed.

Zartan stopped suddenly. Then he apologized and told her it was a bad habit of his. She just rolled her eyes and hoped that Hawk would finish what he needed to do as quickly as possible so she could get away from that weirdo.

"What's on your mind, General?" McCullen asked.

"Securing your warheads," Hawk answered. "A hundred pairs of ears in that room now know when and where they are going to be."

McCullen smiled. "Those 'ears' all have top security clearance," he reminded Hawk.

"We both know what *that's* worth," Hawk said.

McCullen tried to reassure him. "Look, General," he said, "delivery is my responsibility, and it's not one I take lightly. I had NATO assign an elite American Special

Forces unit, a fully armored convoy with air support. I assure you, my warheads will be quite safe."

General Hawk was still skeptical. "If your warheads are half as effective as you say they are, then my team is definitely needed," he said.

"The NATO team's been drilling for weeks," McCullen argued. "They're ready to roll. This is no time for your team to play catch-up."

"My unit doesn't need mission-specific training," Hawk explained. "They're chosen because they can handle any situation, no matter how extreme."

"Maybe next time, General," McCullen said, pretending to be disinterested. But something in his eyes told Hawk that he was *very* interested in the team. "What did you say your unit was called?" he asked.

"I didn't," was Hawk's answer.

McCullen carefully considered this piece of information and nodded his head slowly. He thanked Hawk for his concern and once again promised him that there was nothing to worry about. Then he walked away.

As McCullen left with Zartan, Hawk glanced over at Cover Girl. He flashed her a quick look, and she nodded. Neither of them was willing to take any chances. They both knew that it was time to make sure their team was ready.

ch.2

Deep in the desert, the sun beat down on the gates of MARS Industries' top secret laboratory. Inside, four Special Forces security soldiers escorted two lab workers into the cargo bay. Fifteen more Special Forces soldiers swarmed around three heavily armed transport vehicles. There were two Cougar patrol vehicles armed with state-of-the-art rooftop weapons and one huge Grizzly truck fitted with heavy armor. Duke, the commanding officer, wasn't willing to take any chances. He made sure his team had the firepower to deliver the new nanomite warheads safely.

"All right, listen up!" Duke called out.

The other men stood at attention as Duke began laying out the mission plan.

"The Cougars will be front and back, Grizzly in the

middle carrying the package," he explained. "Minimum distances at all times. Choppers will cover us overhead."

The team quickly jumped into action. As they began double-checking weapons and assignments, the two lab workers approached Duke.

"Captain Hauser," one of them said, walking toward Duke with some forms in hand. Duke took the papers from the man and signed his name. The weapons were now his responsibility.

Ripcord, Duke's second in command and also his best friend, kept his eyes on the lab workers. He watched them for a second before he glanced down at the case holding the warheads. The lab worker handed the case over to Ripcord, who took hold of it very carefully. "Not gonna explode, is it?" he asked with a grin.

"They're not weaponized yet, and the kill switches are inside," the lab worker answered in a deadly serious tone. "All the same, I'd avoid potholes if I were you."

Ripcord smiled again. There wasn't any situation too serious for a joke as far as he was concerned, and he took that as one. He handed the case to his men, and they loaded it onto the Grizzly. "Mount up!" Ripcord hollered, and the assault vehicles roared to life.

Ripcord took the wheel of the lead Cougar with Duke at his side. He hit the gas, and the convoy followed as he drove off the base and into the desert. The hum of two

15

Apache helicopters filled the dawn sky as they swept above the ground vehicles for extra protection. Their guns were at the ready, as were the dual machine guns sitting atop each of the Cougars. Satisfied that everything was in place, Duke radioed headquarters.

"Mother Goose, this is Bird Dog," he said into the radio, using the code names given for the mission. "We have the package and are on the dot to make Ganci Air Base at oh-nine hundred hours."

"Roger that, Bird Dog. Mother Goose out," a voice responded.

Ripcord looked over at Duke. "You know, I hate all the Mother Goose, Bird Dog stuff," he said. "I just wish they'd let us say, 'Hey, Pete, it's Bill.'"

"Not me. I joined up for the jargon," Duke joked.

"Just saying, if I ran things—," Ripcord started to say before Duke cut him off.

"Rip, if you ran the army, things would be a mess!" Then they both laughed in agreement.

Duke had to remind his friend to keep his eyes on the road as the convoy thundered along a winding pass that ran through the mountains. Ripcord gave his buddy a slap on the shoulder and told him to relax. Duke sighed. The steep cliffs all along the road made it hard to relax when Ripcord was taking every turn at top speed.

"You know what I'm thinking about?" Ripcord asked.

Duke sighed again. He knew the answer. There was only one thing Ripcord ever thought about, and it was the last thing Duke wanted to discuss while on the job.

"Please don't say the Air Force," he begged.

"The Air Force," Ripcord said.

"I thought we were done with that discussion."

"*You* were done with it, not me. I love flying!" Ripcord shouted with excitement.

"Look, you want to get up in the air," Duke said. "When we get back to base, I'll buy you a trampoline."

"Funny. Real funny," he said, before getting serious. "Man, we've done ten years in the army; I just think we should see if the grass really is greener."

"I don't want to transfer to the Air Force, okay?" Duke growled. "I don't know how many times I have to tell you."

"It's always about you, isn't it?" Ripcord joked.

"Look, I want to be *in* the fight, not flying over it," Duke told him.

Ripcord looked up at the sky and saw the two Apaches sweeping over him. He'd have given anything to be blazing past them in a superfast jet. "Well, I've got to tell you, my application's all filled out," he said.

Duke smiled. "All filled out?" he asked. "They accept those in crayon?"

The two friends laughed again, completely unaware that a whole lot of trouble was right on their tails.

ch.3

As the convoy sped toward a remote mountain village, a dark shape appeared in the sky behind the helicopters. As it pursued, it kept its distance and stayed off the Cougars' radar screens. But it also stayed close enough to launch an attack at a moment's notice.

In the lead Cougar, Ripcord raced into the village. He remembered it from the test run the team did a few days before. It looked exactly the same, except for one major detail. Last time there were people tending to the cows roaming around. This time the cows were all alone.

"On the training run, weren't there villagers around here?" he asked.

Suddenly suspicious, Duke glanced around. Instantly he was on the alert. He knew a trap when he smelled one, but this time it was too late! The enemy aircraft stormed into position. Its advanced concussion cannons slid out from both sides and poked through the thick exhaust smoke. Before the convoy had time to react, the enemy cannons opened fire. The subatomic blasts punched into the lead Apache, crushing it flat before it exploded.

Duke and Ripcord watched with horror as the ball of flaming metal crashed down in front of them, blocking the road ahead. "Bird down!" Ripcord hollered, slamming on the brakes and bringing the Cougar to a screeching halt.

Duke seized the radio. "Backup! Backup!" he shouted urgently. "Mother Goose, this is Bird Dog. We are under attack. Repeat—we are under attack!"

The remaining Apache swiveled around to face the enemy, a next-generation Typhoon gunship. It hovered in the air on six jet thrusters turned toward the ground and had more firepower than all of the vehicles in the convoy put together.

The Apache unloaded its six-barreled miniguns at the Typhoon, but the rounds bounced off the high-tech armor. Then the Typhoon's concussion cannons returned fire and struck the Apache. The helicopter turned into a flaming ball and spun out of control before it crashed behind the convoy.

With the road blocked at both ends, Duke ordered his team to defend its position. The Grizzly launched two heat-seeking missiles, but the Typhoon gunned them down before they hit the target. Then it opened fire again, this time raining down on the rear Cougar.

The vehicle was flattened instantly!

Another blast from the concussion cannons flipped the Grizzly moments later. Duke watched in the rearview mirror as his team was blown to pieces. Then the Typhoon took aim at them, and Ripcord punched the Cougar into reverse. The blast barely missed, but still hit close enough for the force to launch the reversing Cougar into the air. It flipped end over end several times before it smashed to the ground!

The two soldiers in the back were badly injured. Duke was shaken up, but still in one piece. He quickly checked on Ripcord, nudging him in the side. "You okay?"

Ripcord was dazed, but nodded.

They heard the deafening roar of the Typhoon as it dropped out of the sky and hovered a few feet above the Grizzly.

"What is that?" Ripcord asked.

"*Who* is that?" Duke responded.

They watched as the side door on the Typhoon hissed open. Once the smoke cleared, they saw six menacing soldiers dressed in black battle armor. Each of these Vipers carried a fearsome pulse rifle as they leaped to the ground and spread out, looking for enemy soldiers.

Duke's remaining troops climbed out of the battered Grizzly. They opened fire on the Viper soldiers, but their bullets couldn't penetrate the special armor. The Vipers fired back, and the impact from their more powerful pulse rifles sent the Special Forces soldiers flying.

As the battle raged, another figure stepped out of the Typhoon, but it wasn't another Viper. It was a beautiful woman dressed in skintight body armor. Her face was half hidden behind her midnight-black hair and dark sunglasses. The deadly woman was known as the Baroness, though her real name was Ana. She was a lethal enemy willing to do anything to get what she was after. At that moment she was after the warheads, and she strode toward the burning wreck of the Grizzly, determined to claim her prize.

Duke didn't notice the woman. He was too busy trying to free Ripcord from the wreckage of the Cougar. Duke managed to free his friend moments before the whole thing blew, and the explosion sent them flying in the air. As the Baroness emerged from the Grizzly with the weapons case, she noticed Duke and Ripcord tumbling into a ditch. She drew a pair of pistols from her sides, knowing it wouldn't be long before they came for the case.

Duke rolled over and looked at Ripcord. "Stay here," he warned. "I'm getting that package back." He dashed away, and Ripcord watched on helplessly.

Duke rushed headlong out of the ditch, only to come face-to-face with a Viper's pulse rifle ready to blow him away. Just as Duke was about to meet his fate, the Baroness reached over and clamped her hand down over the barrel. The surprised Viper looked at her, but the Baroness ignored him. She touched the side of her sunglasses and the dark lenses turned clear.

"Hello, Duke," she said.

Duke closed his eyes. He couldn't believe what he had just seen. But when he opened them again, the same familiar face was staring back at him. "Ana?" he asked in complete disbelief.

The Baroness smiled at her old friend, but her smile quickly vanished. A sudden sharp pain shot through the back of her head. She tried to fight it, but it took over. She gave in, took her hand off the gun barrel, and let an evil look sweep across her face. "Good-bye, Duke," she said.

Before the Viper had a chance to fire, a Howler transport ship appeared out of nowhere. The heavily armed aircraft swept into action. The stunned Viper watched as the Howler's four-winged jet thrusters rotated ninety degrees. In a flash it dropped down from the sky and hovered behind Duke.

Duke saw his chance and took it.

He jumped to his feet and knocked the Viper out with one swift punch. Ana didn't waste a second; she turned around and hurried back to the waiting Typhoon.

The Howler's cargo doors opened and a rope dropped out. A ninja dressed in all black slid down. It was Snake Eyes, an elite agent under General Hawk's command. He hit the ground near three Vipers. In a blur he took out two of them with his sword. The third Viper was too far out of his reach, so Snake Eyes drew his pistol and fired. The shot landed between the eye slits of the Viper's helmet and took him out.

Duke watched in awe as the ninja vanished into the gunfire that erupted all around him. Then he pushed himself into action. He took off after the Baroness, keeping his eyes locked on the weapons case in her hands.

A handful of Vipers jumped out from the Typhoon

and opened fire on Duke. The remaining agents in the Howler rushed to help. Scarlett, another one of Hawk's special agents, fast-roped her way down to the ground and pulled out her crossbow pistol. As soon as she got a Viper in her sights, she fired a laserlike arrow bolt. It was a direct hit and ripped through the Viper's armor. She fired at another Viper and took him down as well. It got the Vipers off of Duke's tail as they turned their attention to her.

Enemy fire pinned Scarlett down behind the damaged Grizzly. She was in a tough spot when the Howler touched down. Hershel "Heavy Duty" Dalton, a third agent in Hawk's special unit, leaned out. Only the strongest man in the unit could handle the huge machine gun–grenade launcher that he held in his hands. "Time to lay down some bass!" he shouted, and sprayed grenade fire into the Vipers. With the tables turned, they hurried back to the Typhoon.

The enemy ship whipped around and fired at the Howler. But the Howler was just as advanced and twice as nimble. It fired its side thrusters and rolled onto its side. The blasts from the Typhoon's concussion cannons streaked by harmlessly.

Then Heavy Duty let loose a double blast of hand grenades, but the Typhoon's guns quickly shot them out of the air. Meanwhile, the Howler launched two guided missiles at the Typhoon's cannons. They hit right on target, and the blast ripped the cannons apart.

The Baroness raced toward the Typhoon, hoping to reach it before it was too late.

"Ana!" Duke shouted, charging at her with his pistol drawn. She turned to glance at him just before he tackled her to the ground. During the collision, the case tumbled free, and they both eyed it. Duke sprang into action first, and Heavy Duty took the opportunity to spray gunfire Ana's way.

The Typhoon swept over the Baroness and dropped a rope down to rescue her. Knowing there was no chance to get her hands on the case again, the Baroness decided to save her own life. She grabbed onto the rope and was pulled into the aircraft before it jetted off over the mountains.

Duke seized the weapons case and saw Scarlett, Snake Eyes, and Heavy Duty approaching him. Having no idea who they were, he raised his pistol. The others raised their weapons in response, and Duke yelled at them, "Stand down!"

"Lower your weapon, sir. We're not the enemy," Heavy Duty assured him.

"Pointing weapons at me doesn't make you my friend," Duke argued.

A fourth agent suddenly appeared out of the Howler. The computerized suit he was wearing made him look like a robot. "Please hand over the case, sir," Breaker said politely as he walked toward Duke.

"I don't know who you are!" Duke shouted. He pointed to Scarlett, Snake Eyes, and Heavy Duty, who still had weapons aimed at him. "And I sure don't know who *they* are!" he said, gesturing toward the Vipers. "Until I find out, I'm not lowering anything or handing anything over."

The sudden click of a rifle caused everyone to glance behind them. Ripcord had climbed out of the ditch to cover his friend's back. Feeling like the odds had turned in their favor, Ripcord started asking the questions. "What's your unit?" he demanded.

"That's classified," Scarlett answered. Out of the corners of her eyes, she saw Snake Eyes reaching for the ninja throwing stars attached to his suit. She gave him a look, signaling him to stop. After all, they were all on the same side, even if Duke and Ripcord didn't know it yet.

Breaker carefully took a small device from his pocket. He showed Duke that it wasn't a weapon. It was only a piece of communication equipment known as a holo-projector. "Someone would like a word with you," Breaker said, setting the device on the ground.

The device sent out a flash of light, which quickly changed into a 3-D projection of General Hawk. "State your name and rank," Hawk's image ordered.

Duke was almost too stunned to reply. "You first," was all he managed to stutter out.

"My team just saved your life, son," Hawk reminded him. "Now's the part where you say 'thank you.'"

"Those aren't the words that come to mind just now," Duke growled. "I wasn't told about any support for this mission, so you better tell *your* team to stand down."

Ripcord kept his rifle aimed and ready. "I'd be happy to turn this into a turkey shoot," he told Duke.

"Easy . . . Ripcord," General Hawk's projection said, reading off a file. Ripcord glanced at the holo-projector and wondered how it knew his name.

"I'm General Clayton Abernathy," Hawk said. "You may have heard of me . . . Duke."

Duke was caught off guard, and Breaker saw an opening. He stepped closer to Duke and swept a scanner across the weapons case. Snapping out of his surprise, Duke swiveled his gun around and held it to Breaker's head.

"I just need to deactivate the tracking beacon, for security," Breaker calmly explained. Duke pulled the gun away but kept his aim steady, just in case.

General Hawk wanted to put an end to the standoff. He asked Duke again to hand over the case. "Let us deliver the warheads," he said.

"No way," Duke snapped. "My mission, my package. *I* carry them; *I* deliver them."

"Fine," Hawk said. He realized he wasn't going to change Duke's mind. "But you seem to be a little short on transportation at the moment." His holo-image nodded in the direction of the destroyed vehicles littering the road. "Team Alpha will deliver you to me."

Duke realized that General Hawk had a point. He wouldn't get very far in two blown-up Cougars. "Where exactly are *you*, sir?" he asked.

"Come see for yourself," Hawk said.

"All right," Duke agreed.

In less than a minute everyone had boarded the Howler. When it took off, Duke and Ripcord were safely aboard with the weapons case tucked between them.

ch.5

As the Howler flew toward Egypt, Scarlett bandaged the head wound Ripcord had suffered when the Cougar crashed. He watched her as she carefully cleaned the scrapes. It hadn't taken long for him to know he was in love, and he winked at her. His mood had definitely lightened up now that it was clear these guys weren't the enemy.

"Hey, you're cute," he said.

Heavy Duty shook his head and laughed. "You don't want to call her cute," he warned.

"Yeah, man," Breaker agreed. "Don't call her cute."

Snake Eyes came up to Ripcord with a sharp needle, but Ripcord was too busy staring at Scarlett to notice. He was caught off guard by the pinch from the shot and had to bite his lip to keep from screaming in pain.

"I thought all you special ops guys were tough," Scarlett teased as Ripcord moaned.

"We are tough. But we're also sensitive," Ripcord told her as he rubbed his arm.

Duke hadn't quite relaxed as much as his friend. He still kept a tight hold on the weapons case and an eye open for any suspicious behavior. "What kind of outfit is this?" he asked. "Not regular army, that's for sure."

"We'd get tossed out for telling," Scarlett said.

"Duke, don't you get it?" Ripcord said. "They're supersecret, like something out of the movies."

Duke nodded. He got it. The truth was, he didn't really care so much *who* they were; he just wanted to know what their next step was. "You're gonna go after them, aren't you? The ones that hit my convoy." No one answered, but they didn't need to. Duke knew they were, because that's what his Special Forces would do. "I want in," he said.

"Not our call," Heavy Duty said as the Howler approached their base.

The unit's base wasn't like any other Duke and Ripcord had ever seen. It was buried deep under the sand of the Egyptian desert and was known only as the Pit. Inside, the security forces watched as the Howler approached on their computer screens. They cleared the ship for landing and opened the hatch doors. The Howler hovered for a moment as the sand dune directly below spiraled open and revealed an underground platform.

General Hawk waited for the Howler to touch down. He approached the landing doors and greeted Scarlett with a nod. Duke and Ripcord were close behind. Their eyes darted back and forth as they scanned the impressive base.

"Welcome to the Pit," Hawk greeted them. He closed the file he'd been reading and handed it over to Cover Girl. "I've read a lot about you two," he said to Duke. "Matter of fact, I saw that one of my men tried to recruit you to our little operation a while back."

Duke raised his eyebrows and tilted his head. "I was never asked to join any op group." Hawk grinned and asked Duke if he remembered talking to a tall man in Thailand four years ago. Duke searched his memory, then nodded. "Yeah," he said, but wasn't convinced.

"Four years ago, my boy had issues," Ripcord said, trying to cover for his friend's lack of recollection.

Duke quickly changed the subject. He didn't want to talk about four years ago. He was concerned with what was going to happen next. "Anyway, this doesn't look like any base I've ever seen. Where exactly are we?" he asked.

"Okay, you trusted me," Hawk told him. "I'll trust you."

Hawk gave a signal, and the platform under their feet

began to move. It started to go down like an elevator, passing different training floors as it went. The first level it passed was an urban combat level. The entire floor was a replica of a city that stretched out as far as Duke could see. The buildings, the cars . . . Everything was laid out exactly like a real city—except that the men and women who were training there were using next-generation weapons that Duke and Ripcord had only imagined.

"Technically, G.I. JOE doesn't exist," explained Hawk. "But if it did, it'd be made up of the top men and women from the best military units all over the world. Ten nations signed on in the first year. Working together and sharing intel. Now we have twenty-three nations."

On the training floor, a woman zipped by wearing a camo-suit that reflected light and made her nearly invisible. As she moved along, she blended into the changing background.

"Oh man, I want one of those," Ripcord said.

"Camouflage suit," Heavy Duty told him.

"Liquid armor," Scarlett added.

"I've never seen combat gear like this," Duke said. He shook his head in awe. This outfit was definitely above and beyond any he'd ever worked with before.

The elevator passed several more training floors before it stopped. Then Hawk led the group into the control room, where dozens of men monitored the many computers that were set up there. One of them came up to Hawk as he entered and informed him that he had Mr. McCullen standing by on the holo-projector.

"Patch him through," Hawk said.

As they waited, Duke asked if they knew who had attacked them.

"Currently unidentified," Cover Girl said. "But whoever that woman was, she's clearly well financed, with access to highly classified information and state-of-the-art weaponry."

"We need to find out everything we can about her," Hawk said. "Knowing is half the battle."

Duke kept a steady face. Until he knew more, he wasn't going to let on that he had plenty of information about the Baroness.

As Hawk finished speaking, McCullen's image suddenly appeared; a ring of cameras allowed his projection to move freely throughout the control room. Hawk introduced him to everyone and explained that McCullen was the man whose company built the warheads inside the case that Duke was still holding.

"General, seems I was wrong," McCullen admitted, turning toward Hawk. "*Clearly* you were the security option I should have chosen."

Duke took this as a personal affront and told McCullen that his team did everything they could. "That mission was classified." He sneered. *"Clearly,* somebody sold us out!"

McCullen wasn't used to being spoken to like that by anyone. His face twisted into an angry expression. "Your job, Captain, was to protect those warheads," he barked. "If it wasn't for General Hawk, you would've failed."

Duke groaned but knew better than to say anything more.

McCullen then asked Hawk for their current coordinates. He was going to send another NATO team to get the warheads, but this time it would be a larger, better-armed force.

Hawk shook his head. He wasn't going to risk another disaster. "It's not that I don't trust *you,"* he told McCullen. "I don't trust *anybody."*

"Are you sure you're not a McCullen?" McCullen joked.

"I don't talk smooth enough to be a McCullen," Hawk told him.

They shared a quick smile before getting back to business. McCullen explained to the other agents that they needed to disable the tracking device so that the people who attacked them wouldn't be able to find them again. Breaker assured him that it was already done, and McCullen seemed happy. "Good," he said. "So, can I count on you to deliver the warheads to NATO now?" he asked Hawk.

"I think it's unwise to move them right now," Hawk said. "This group that attacked us might make another attempt. We need to find them before we can consider moving your weapons."

"All right," McCullen agreed reluctantly. "But at least let me check the warheads to see if any have been damaged." Breaker assured him that he had already checked, but McCullen wanted him to double-check. Duke set the case down, and Breaker used the eyepiece on his suit to scan the case.

"My scan says they're intact," Breaker informed them.

But this wasn't enough proof for McCullen. He wanted to see with his own holographic eyes. He gave Hawk the code to unlock the case and asked him to open it. Then his projection moved in close and ran his fingers over the warheads. Once satisfied, he told Hawk to keep him informed. Then his image vanished.

Once McCullen was gone, Breaker turned to the rest of the team. Breaker was scanning the man's image the entire time. "That bloke's Beta Waves were going up, down, and sideways," he said. "He's hiding something."

McCullen paced back and forth inside the Trident submarine as it cut through the ocean. His anger was boiling over, and the crew stayed out of his way. "I spent five years setting this up!" he yelled. "*This* was supposed to be the easy part!"

In her flickering holo-projection form, Ana narrowed her eyes at McCullen. She'd spent months arguing with him over the details of the raid, and blamed him for the flawed plan. "If you'd let me stage the assault at your precious factory, we could have contained the situation," she said.

"And lose the trust of our clients?" he snapped, shaking his head. The attack needed to look like it was NATO's fault, not MARS Industries'. Besides, he didn't believe the plan was the problem. He blamed Ana for not taking out Duke and escaping with the case when she had the chance. "What happened? Did you hesitate?"

"Are you implying this is about some ancient history between me and Duke? That's as laughable as your intel," Ana told him. "What went wrong was a support team appearing out of nowhere."

McCullen stared harshly at her for a moment. But he never could stay angry with Ana for too long, and soon his expression softened. "Forgive me," he said. "Jealousy isn't my strong suit."

"Forget about that," the Baroness told him. There were more important things to worry about—for instance, where the warheads were at that moment. "Have you tracked the case?"

McCullen flashed an evil grin. "They deactivated the beacon," he said. "But I gave them a code to quietly reactivate it." The code he'd given Hawk to open the case had secretly turned the beacon back on. McCullen eyed the monitor in front of him, following the blinking dot smack in the middle of the Egyptian desert. "There it is. The Pit. I'd bet anything," he said.

"The Pit?" Ana asked.

"The base of operations for an elite international unit that's only mentioned in whispers," explained McCullen. Then he sent the coordinates to Ana and explained that she'd find the warheads there. As her holo-form blinked off, another one stepped up behind McCullen.

"If you had sent me in the first place, it would already be done," the well-dressed holo-image of a man whispered.

"I'm sending you now, Storm Shadow," McCullen told him. "There can be no more mistakes. The schedule must not be compromised any further." Storm Shadow's projection nodded once before it vanished.

McCullen glanced out the submarine's observation window as it slowly approached a massive facility built safely under the polar ice caps. This multilevel underwater complex was the secret headquarters of MARS Industries and was impossible to find by radar. But in case anyone ever did stumble on it, several harpoon guns and a fearsome turbo-pulse cannon were installed to defend the base. Even though he'd designed this marvel of modern technology, McCullen still couldn't help but be impressed.

The Trident submarine docked. When the watertight doors opened, McCullen strode onto the platform. He saw the man known as the Doctor waiting for his arrival.

"Welcome back," the Doctor's mechanically engineered voice remarked. He wore a life-support mask that covered his face and mechanically pumped air into his lungs. "We've been very busy."

The Doctor drew McCullen's attention to twenty men standing nearby. These soldiers were standing perfectly still—not a single muscle flinched. They were part of the Doctor's latest experiment. He referred to them as Neo Vipers, a far superior model of the clan's current soldiers.

"Is it working?" McCullen asked.

The Doctor was only too eager to demonstrate the progress he had made. He waved over his shoulder, and one of his lab assistants brought over a glass case containing a giant king cobra snake. "The king cobra is a magnificent creature. Its venom can kill a full-grown elephant with a single bite," the Doctor said as he walked over to one of the Neo Vipers and pointed to a small scar behind the right ear.

He explained how each Neo Viper was injected with a nanomite solution. The nanomites then destroyed part of the Viper's brain cortex and left them completely brainwashed.

"They feel no fear," the Doctor said. "And they feel no pain."

He commanded the Neo Viper to reach into the cobra tank and squeeze the deadly snake. The Neo Viper obeyed without hesitation, and the cobra instantly latched onto his arm. As the snake sank its venomous fangs into his veins, the Neo Viper didn't even wince.

The Neo Viper released the snake only after being ordered. He dropped to his knees shortly after, suffering from the effects of the poison. McCullen looked concerned, but the Doctor told him not to worry. "The nanomites will target the venom," he said.

Within seconds the Neo Viper was back on his feet. McCullen was extremely impressed. "You've done well," he said.

The Doctor informed him that one unit was already in place. He promised to have more soon, but reminded McCullen that this kind of science was very expensive. "If I could make a suggestion," he said, "selling one batch of warheads on the black market would cover our costs."

"No," McCullen said firmly. "This world is messy enough. What it needs is unification. Leadership. It needs to be taken out of chaos by someone with complete control. Once I get my hands on the reins, the money will take care of itself."

McCullen's plan to take control of the world was already shaping up. He led the Doctor into an operating chamber where Zartan was being scanned by a fleet of computerized robots. Zartan was a master of disguise and had been studying for weeks, preparing for his part in the master plan. The Doctor knew little about Zartan's role, only that the robots were programmed to change Zartan's fingerprints. But as he listened to McCullen, he started putting the pieces together, and smiled.

If McCullen's plan was half as devious as the Doctor suspected, the world would be in for a big shock!

In the Pit's control room, Duke stared up at the monitor. The photo of Ana, which Breaker had snapped with his helmet cam during the assault, was staring back at him. Duke kept an intense focus on the image as Ripcord came up behind him. "Hey, isn't that—," Ripcord whispered, but Duke cut him off with quick look.

Breaker punched a few keys on the keyboard, and another image popped up next to Ana's. A continuous flow of women's photos appeared and disappeared beside Ana's as the computer searched databases across the world for a match for Breaker's snapshot.

"We have access to any photograph on any server anywhere in the world," Cover Girl remarked to Duke and Ripcord.

"Everyone gets photographed at some time," Breaker said. "ATMs, airports, crowd shots at a football game."

"We'll find her. Then we'll work up the chain and find who sent her," Hawk assured his team, not knowing Duke could save them all the trouble.

Ripcord continued to stare at the photo, but he followed Duke's lead and kept his mouth shut. If his commanding officer was keeping Ana's identity a secret, so would he.

Cover Girl caught Hawk's attention and let him know a communication was coming in from NATO. She gave Hawk a handheld computer so he could read the message. He turned to Duke once he'd finished. "Duke, your mission is complete," he said. "NATO has appointed me the official custodian of the warheads."

Duke nodded his head and handed the case over with a hint of defeat. He wasn't ready to back out of the fight. "She's gonna come after you," he said. "You know that, right?"

"And your point is?" Hawk asked him.

"You're going to go after her first," Duke answered. "And I want in."

"Yeah, let us in on this, sir!" Ripcord said, also ready for action. "Our team just got wasted. I think we deserve a little payback."

Hawk narrowed his eyes at the pair. "You don't ask to be part of G.I. JOE," he said. "You *get* asked."

Duke knew the general wouldn't give in easily, so he played the ace up his sleeve. "I know her," he said, pointing to Ana's picture. "You said knowing is half the battle. Well, I know who she is."

Duke reached into his pocket, pulled out a photograph, and showed it to Hawk. The general studied the picture carefully. It was clearly a photo of Duke and the woman who attacked the convoy. She looked different, though. There was no hint of evil hidden behind her eyes in the photograph Duke had.

"Her name is Ana Lewis, and I can tell you everything you need to know about her up until . . . four years ago," Duke told Hawk. "After that, well, obviously a lot's changed."

Hawk shook his head, amazed by this twist of fate, but he was willing to listen. And if it meant bringing Duke and Ripcord aboard the team, Hawk was okay with doing that, too. However, before it went any further, he needed to know he could trust them.

Hawk could easily tell from the picture that Duke and Ana were in love. Obviously something must have happened between them. "I need to know what I'm dealing with: a man who can put the mission first or a man looking to settle a score," Hawk said. Then he paused for a moment before he asked Duke the question he really needed to know the answer to: "Could you kill her?"

Four years before, Duke never would've considered the question. But after the battle earlier that day, the answer was as clear as the sky. "If I had to," he said.

"Chances are you will," Hawk warned him. "And unless you can kill her—graveyard dead—I don't want you."

"I can," Duke answered without a second thought.

Hawk eyed him carefully for a moment before he was convinced that Duke was telling the truth. "Okay," he said. "So tell me about her."

The sports car's headlights cut through the Paris streets before it raced up the driveway of a magnificent mansion. The car sped to a stop, and the engine died down. When the driver's door opened, the Baroness stepped out.

The servants waited at the door and took Ana's coat as she entered. She tossed it off without even glancing at them. In the few short years she'd been married to Baron Leon DeCobray, Ana had learned to enjoy the privileges of being extremely rich.

As soon as he heard the car pull up, the Baron strode into the entrance hall, waiting to give his wife a welcome-home kiss. As far as he knew, Ana had been on vacation. He'd missed her very much. Lately he'd been so busy working in his lab on a classified government project that they hadn't seen much of each other in weeks.

"How is work at the lab?" Ana asked him after they hugged.

"Steady progress," DeCobray told her. "You know I wish I could tell you more."

"Of course," Ana said. She understood the need for secrecy more than her husband imagined.

"How were the shops in Monte Carlo?"

Ana shrugged. "I didn't get what I was after," she said.

"I suppose I should be grateful," the Baron joked, thinking of the money he'd saved. Ana smiled. She let him hang onto the silly notions he had about her life.

After a moment the couple headed up the grand staircase and entered her enormous bedroom. The Baroness went over to the large double doors that led to the balcony. She threw them open, taking in the incredible view of the Eiffel Tower. "I never get over how beautiful . . . ," she said. She let her words trail off as something caught her attention. She took a closer look and saw Storm Shadow perched near the entrance to the room.

Ana quickly spun around and pulled her husband close to distract him. She knew Storm Shadow wouldn't hesitate to kill DeCobray to protect their secret identities. "Let me change and freshen up," she said to her husband. "Then I'll meet you for dinner."

"Of course," the Baron said, smiling at her before he left.

Ana smiled, too, but it faded as soon as DeCobray exited. She spun back around in a flash and rushed over to Storm Shadow. She demanded to know what he was doing there.

"Mr. McCullen gave me orders," he said.

The Baroness sighed. She knew all about McCullen's orders. He was a very jealous man and didn't approve of her marriage one bit. Ana told him a million times that it was only for the mission, but McCullen still felt the need to spy on her. The only reason he put up with DeCobray at all was because his research was going to benefit MARS Industries.

"I'll be coming with you to retrieve the warheads—along with some of the men the Doctor's been working on," Storm Shadow informed Ana.

Ana shuddered at the mention of the Doctor. She didn't care how valuable his work was; she wished McCullen would get rid of that freak.

"We go at dawn," Storm Shadow told her in Korean. Ana understood and nodded. She'd be ready.

She waited for Storm Shadow to disappear before moving. Once she was alone, she went over to her dresser and opened a hidden drawer. She took a small box from the compartment and opened it carefully. The dim light from the lamp behind her caught the diamonds on the engagement ring inside and made it sparkle like a star. The sight of the ring brought a flood of memories back to Ana as she stood, staring.

It was hard for her to believe it had only been four years ago, on a balcony in Washington, DC, when she'd first set eyes on the ring. It was Duke's last night before shipping out, and they'd spent the entire evening together. He'd waited until the end of the night to drop to his knee and surprise her with the ring.

"I've been wanting to do this before we deploy," he told her. She remembered how happy she was at that moment, then realized that was the last night she'd ever felt that way. It was the last night she was together with Duke, and it was also the last time she saw her brother, Rex, alive.

She promised to marry Duke as long as he promised to take care of Rex on the mission they were shipping off for in the morning. It was Rex's first combat mission as an army scientist, and she was worried. She trusted Duke to take care of him. But he wasn't able to keep that promise, and she never kept hers. Staring at the ring again, the lights of Paris behind her in the distance, Ana wondered what her life would have been like if they'd both kept their word.

Back in the Pit, Heavy Duty showed Duke and Ripcord G.I. JOE's latest piece of armor. It was called an Accelerator Suit—made of tough titanium, enhanced with head-to-toe hydraulics, and complete with computerized helmets. The suit helped agents run faster, jump higher, and take more of a beating.

Duke and Ripcord buckled into their suits, ready for training.

"It's my job to get you mission ready, JOE style," Heavy Duty said as he explained all the special features of the suit to the new recruits. He pointed out the firepower, showing them the submachine guns and the six heat-seeking missiles.

"Fully self-contained firepower," he said. "Perfect

for a couple of cowboys like you."

Ripcord glanced away from the gadgets on the suit and looked over at Heavy Duty. "I just missed everything you said," Ripcord said. Heavy Duty told him not worry about it. He said Ripcord would figure it out soon enough, and led them into the urban combat level that they'd passed earlier on their way into the base.

They put the suits to the test right away as they ran through an explosive obstacle course at full speed. Duke and Ripcord dodged sniper fire and avoided explosions on their way through. Both of them successfully navigated the course and punched fists in celebration.

One of the G.I. JOE lieutenants, Lt. Stone, went over to watch them. He rode through the combat zone on his attack cycle, obviously impressed with the two new recruits. "Are they JOEs?" he asked Heavy Duty as he pulled alongside him.

"Not yet," Heavy Duty told him, but he sounded confident that they would be soon. Duke and Ripcord had many more training exercises to complete before that could happen. And Stone wasted no time putting them to the test.

Starting with hand-to-hand combat training, Duke was matched up against Snake Eyes. The two men faced off, armed with electrified jousting sticks. Snake Eyes, a master of martial arts, easily knocked Duke down as Stone and Heavy Duty observed.

Duke sprang back to his feet. "Again," he said, determined not to give up. He fought courageously but couldn't hold off the world's greatest ninja. Stone winced as Duke hit the ground with a thud for a second time, but Duke jumped right back up. "Again!"

Duke was more aggressive the next time. He performed a great reverse move and got a solid hit on Snake Eyes. The impact actually knocked Snake Eyes back a few steps.

Breaker's mouth dropped open as he watched. "I have never *ever* seen Snake Eyes take a hit!"

Meanwhile, Ripcord was busy with a different test. Smack in the middle of the training city, he waited for a buzzer to sound. Once it did, he'd have sixty seconds to eliminate the enemy targets that popped up all around him.

Just as he was about to rush in, he glanced over and gave Scarlett a wink. "Just so you know," he told her, "when I get a target in my sights, I take it down." Then the buzzer sounded, and he ran headlong into the action. Rolling, diving, and firing away, Ripcord cleared the floor of targets. And when the sixty-second timer went off, he threw a big grin Scarlett's way.

"You missed one," she said, unimpressed.

"Gimme a break," Ripcord pleaded.

"If you're going to shoot at something, kill it," she said firmly. "Otherwise take up knitting." She walked off with a mischievous smile on her lips, passing Heavy Duty, who had just checked the box on his clipboard marked PASS.

Stone grinned. "So, they JOEs?" he asked again.

"Might be," Heavy Duty said before he headed off to deliver the test results to General Hawk. The rest of the team waited in the workout room, lifting weights and getting to know one another a little better.

Once Hawk stepped in, though, everyone stopped talking and came to attention. He held the final results of all the tests in his hands. "Duke, you scored in the top half percent of all people we've ever tested," he said. Stone patted Duke on the back and congratulated him as Ripcord waited for his results. "Ripcord . . . well, if we average your score with Duke's, you pass too," Hawk teased before he officially welcomed the two recruits to G.I. JOE.

Breaker, Scarlett, Snake Eyes, and Heavy Duty all gathered around them and raised their fists in the air. "YO, JOE!" they cheered.

"We still need to see if you pass in the field," Heavy Duty warned.

Duke and Ripcord weren't worried about that. If there's one place they'd proven their worth a million times, it was in battle.

As the team celebrated, the Pit's security room buzzed with action. On the infrared monitors, the workers watched a man and his herd of camels walk across the sand dunes high above. After an X-ray scan revealed nothing suspicious, the security team lost interest.

A moment later the monitors flashed as several strange readings sprang up around the herd. "Sensors are detecting seismic activity," one of the security officers reported.

"Probably just a tremor, but let's have a team check it out," another said. But before they had a chance to do anything, the radar blips suddenly dived down toward the image of the base. Realizing that these were vehicles, not tremors, the officer rushed to sound the alarm, but it was too late. The Mole Pod machines were already drilling through the thick rock walls of the Pit.

The outer wall on the urban combat level crumbled as ten Mole Pods crashed through. The doors to the digging vehicles slid open, and the Baroness stepped out. Storm Shadow, Zartan, and seven Neo Vipers quickly joined her and spread out to cover the grounds. Ana pulled out a high-tech scanning device. It beamed out a 3-D graphic of the Pit, showing all the levels and the people moving about them. She pointed the way down the tunnel that led directly to the warheads.

Storm Shadow ordered some of the Neo Vipers to guard the Mole Pods as he and the rest of the assault team hurried away. An alert G.I. JOE agent crept up behind them, but nothing escaped Storm Shadow's glare. He took out the agent without any effort, and the team continued on its way.

Unaware of the attack, General Hawk returned to his office. Cover Girl gave him a computerized tablet that contained pages of electronic forms for him to sign. Neither of them had any idea that they were being watched.

"Anything else?" Hawk asked, and handed the tablet back to her. Cover Girl didn't have time to answer; a sword suddenly stabbed the tablet. Hawk reached for his pistol, but Storm Shadow buried his sword into Hawk's gut before he could fire. Cover Girl gasped as the general collapsed.

With a quick blow to her head, Zartan knocked out Cover Girl. Ana hurried over and ripped Hawk's security badge off his jacket. She swiped it across the lock of the vault door, and Storm Shadow pulled Hawk's face up to the eye scanner. The vault slipped opened, revealing the weapons case sitting inside.

Back in the workout room, Duke and the rest of the G.I. JOE agents propelled themselves up as the base's alarm blared to life. "The warheads!" Duke yelled. He had known it would be only a matter of time before the enemy tried to steal them again.

They headed for the urban training level and reached it just as Ana and Storm Shadow arrived with the weapons case. "Prepare the machines," Ana ordered the Neo Vipers over the com-link that connected her earpiece with theirs.

As the Neo Vipers turned to do what they were told, Heavy Duty launched a grenade at them. Ana and Storm Shadow watched helplessly from a walkway above as the explosion killed them all and destroyed the Mole Pods instantly. The Baroness quick-drew her pulse pistols and blasted away at Heavy Duty. He dived for cover just in time but lost his weapon in the shuffle.

Safe for the moment, Ana and Storm Shadow searched for another way out. Storm Shadow spotted a pair of jet packs mounted on a rack thirty feet below. "Follow me," he said, and jumped over the railing. Ana blasted her way down instead. She shot the walkway in front of her and created a slide that took her within feet of Storm Shadow.

As they strapped on the jet packs, Duke rushed up to them with his guns raised. "Put the case down, Ana!" he hollered.

Both Storm Shadow and Ana froze. As Duke stepped closer, she saw a Neo Viper sneak in behind him. To buy some time, she pretended to cooperate. "Fine," she said, and placed the case on the ground. "Done."

Just then the Neo Viper took aim. He was about to pull the trigger when something rushed at him. He turned around and saw Ripcord driving a forklift on a collision course. The forklift smashed into the Neo Viper and crushed him instantly.

Ana used the diversion to take a step closer to Duke.

"Stop right there," Duke warned, but she kept walking closer and closer.

"You can't shoot me, can you?" she asked.

"I will if I have to," Duke promised.

"Deep down, you still love me," she said.

"Don't listen to her, Duke!" Ripcord shouted as Duke cocked his pistol.

"Don't make me do this," he begged as she took another step, coming face-to-face with him. Storm Shadow crept closer, too, so Duke leveled the pistol at Ana's forehead. "Move and I'll blow her away," he warned Storm Shadow.

At that moment another Neo Viper charged at Duke, and was preparing to shoot when he noticed the forklift coming right at him. He fired a pulse blast, and all the metal plates were torn off the forklift. Ripcord ducked, dodging the flying metal. He popped back up at the wheel and drove the forklift right into the Neo Viper.

As the Neo Viper fell back, his pulse pistol went off. The blast landed above Duke and knocked him to the ground. The Baroness grabbed the case in a flash and ran toward the elevator platform. Ripcord flung himself off the mangled forklift and charged after her. Storm Shadow lunged at him, slicing Ripcord's pistol in half with a swipe from one of his two swords. Storm Shadow was about to strike Ripcord with the other sword when the blade clashed with another; Snake Eyes had flown in between them.

The two ninja warriors erupted into battle. Their swords flashed at impossible speeds, deflecting the other's attack until their blades finally locked. As they faced off, Snake Eyes glanced over at his enemy's right arm. Right away he noticed the same red markings that were tattooed on his own arm. It suddenly dawned on him that they were so evenly matched because they were from the same ninja clan.

"Hello, brother," Storm Shadow growled. His words caught Snake Eyes off guard, and Storm Shadow took the opportunity to elbow Snake Eyes in the face, knocking him to the ground before he vanished into the smoke from a nearby blast.

The remaining Neo Vipers opened fire and pinned both Duke and Ripcord down. As the fire fight raged, Ana leaped onto the rising elevator. Dressed in the high-tech camo-suit, Scarlett chased after her and followed Ana onto the elevator. As the elevator rose toward the ground level, Scarlett kicked the pistol from Ana's hand. The two women began to battle viciously, and the weapons case went flying. It landed on a ramp below, and they both tumbled after it.

Ana drew her other pistol and took aim. Scarlett switched on the camo-suit and disappeared right in front of Ana's eyes. Ana fired at the ripples of air around her, but the shots missed their mark. Seconds later Scarlett landed a blow that disarmed Ana of her other pistol.

The rest of the G.I. JOE agents had their hands full, fighting off the Neo Vipers. Each time they thought the Neo Vipers were done for, they staggered back to their feet and attacked again. In a last-ditch attempt to clear a path to the elevator platform, Ripcord unloaded a rocket launcher on the enemy. The blast sent debris shooting across the entire floor and got the job done. There was only one Neo Viper left in their way.

Duke charged at him, firing blast after blast from his shotgun. Ana saw him getting closer. She had to get away before the team caught up with her, so she desperately grabbed a nearby oil pan and flung the oil in all directions. The liquid sprayed everything, including Scarlett, and made her visible. Ana jumped on her and knocked her to the ground.

Not far away, Storm Shadow ignited the jet pack strapped to his back. He rocketed toward Ana, leaving a trail of blue light shooting out of the engine pack. He grabbed Ana by the arm, and the two swept down to the ramp where the weapons case was resting, ready for the taking.

Duke hurried but got there a split second after them. The Baroness already had the case in hand, and she nailed Duke in the head with one swing. Duke tumbled backward and fell into the elevator shaft. He caught hold of a metal bar and saved himself just in time to see Storm Shadow and Ana rocketing toward the Pit's secret hatch.

Ana took Storm Shadow's pulse gun and blasted it at the hatch's heavy doors. They exploded in a ball of fire, and Ana and Storm Shadow flew up through the hole and into a waiting Typhoon gunship that hovered overhead.

From the desert sand, Zartan watched the Typhoon as it sped away. He quickly glanced behind him at the dead herdsman on the ground. Safely disguised, he walked away from the smoking battle with the herdsman's camels following closely behind. As always, he preferred the sneaky way out of a fight.

As the other G.I. JOE agents cleaned up the mess the battle had left, Snake Eyes sat by himself. Deep in thought, he hadn't moved in the hours since the fight ended. The encounter with Storm Shadow had surprised and stunned him. His memories flashed back to a time when he was ten years old and lived on the streets of Tokyo.

His martial arts training had begun there one rainy night. Scared and hungry, he waited outside a temple and peered into the kitchen. Once the room was empty, he sneaked in and started eating from a pot of rice on the counter. He'd only taken one bite when another boy caught him and came at him with a kitchen knife.

"Thief!" the boy shouted, swinging the knife as he tried to cut the young Snake Eyes to pieces.

Snake Eyes used every one of his street-fighting skills to avoid being stabbed. But even so, it didn't take long for the other boy to pin him down. If the temple's headmaster hadn't come to his rescue, that first battle with Storm Shadow would've been his last.

As it turned out, the headmaster spotted the boy's natural talent. Snake Eyes was invited to stay and train with the other boys at the temple. However, the hatred between him and the boy who attacked him only grew. That fight had flared up again in the Pit, and Snake Eyes was angry with himself for letting Storm Shadow get the best of him yet again.

Snake Eyes wasn't the only one disappointed in himself. The entire G.I. JOE team was upset for getting caught off guard on their home turf. Scarlett still couldn't believe what had happened. No one before had ever gotten the jump on her the way Ana had, and she felt responsible for letting the case get away. Ripcord tried to make her feel better. He let her know it wasn't her fault. Scarlett refused to listen, though. She knew the attack wasn't her fault, but letting them get away was. With the missiles in enemy hands, it meant all the G.I. JOE agents who had been killed had lost their lives in vain. But for the sake of the mission, she did her best to put it out of her mind. The mission always came first.

Duke also struggled with his own guilt as he looked

at Hawk, who was hooked up to a life-support machine in the Pit's sick bay. The machine recorded Hawk's faint but steady heartbeat as the medic bandaged Duke's wounded shoulder.

Duke couldn't shake the image of Ana as she fought Scarlett. There was pure evil in Ana's eyes. All traces of the woman he used to love had vanished, yet he still wasn't able to pull the trigger when he needed to. He'd promised Hawk that he'd be able to, and he'd let the general down. Because of him, Ana had secured the warheads and Hawk was fighting for his life.

"That ought to hold you," the medic said as he finished the bandage.

Duke thanked him and then returned to his thoughts. Ana's evil stare flashed across his mind. He convinced himself that next time he'd be able to do what needed to be done. He'd be able to kill her—graveyard dead—like he'd promised.

★ ★ ★

Meanwhile, the mood at McCullen's underwater base was vastly different. He was very pleased with the job Ana and Storm Shadow had done. With the warheads in his possession, McCullen was one step closer to world domination. "Take the warheads to Paris and have them weaponized," McCullen ordered his two agents' holo-projections. "Then I want you to test one."

"Test one?" Ana asked, surprised at the change in plan. They'd never talked about actually using the weapons, only threatening to use them.

But McCullen had a different idea in mind. "We'll show everyone how well they perform," he said with a twisted grin.

Storm Shadow agreed with this new course of action. "Fear is a great motivator," he said. It was a lesson he had learned as a boy and used often.

McCullen wandered across the control room and gazed at an iron mask resting in a glass case. It was the one James McCullen was forced to wear hundreds of years ago. Finally he would get revenge for the horrible punishment his ancestor had had to endure. "I have a target in mind," McCullen told Storm Shadow and Ana. "One the French will never forget— as I have never forgotten what the French did to my ancestor."

He sent them the target coordinates and dismissed them. Their holographic images disappeared, and it was time for the second phase of his plan. Destro McCullen left the control room and headed for the operating room. Zartan had returned to the base, and was about to undergo the second phase of the complicated procedure that the robots had started earlier. McCullen had brought the Doctor onboard with the plan and wanted him to perform the final operation.

Zartan was sitting on the operating table when

McCullen arrived to oversee the process.

"Are you ready, Mr. Zartan?" the Doctor asked.

"Born ready," Zartan said with a smile. "Eighteen months of studying my target, learning his manners, adopting his eating habits . . . This is going to be the achievement of a lifetime."

"Gentlemen," McCullen interrupted, having lost his patience. "Let's get it going."

"Once I have my money," Zartan said with the sly air of a businessman. McCullen told him the money should be in his account by now. Zartan checked, punched a few keys on his handheld computer, and nodded. "Ah! The transfer just hit my account," he said. "Party time."

The Doctor stepped up and strapped him down. The computerized robots swarmed around Zartan, injecting him with dozens of long needles. Then a larger needle moved in and made an incision behind Zartan's right ear. The injection quickly fed thousands of nanomites into his bloodstream.

Zartan screamed as his eyes bulged and he fought against his restraints. He struggled to get free as the nanomites reshaped his bones. His facial features changed in the blink of an eye, and the Doctor grinned proudly. With the operation complete, no one would be able to tell Zartan apart from the man he'd been programmed to resemble.

McCullen's evil plan had just taken another huge leap forward.

Hard Drive

COBRA Files

PIT Data

Network

e Files

uiting

Trash

Hard Drive

COBRA Files

ata

rk

Case Files

Recruiting

Trash

Hard Drive

COBRA Files

PIT Data

Network

Case Files

Recruiting

Trash

Hard Drive

COBRA Files

PIT Data

Trash

The body of a Neo Viper rested lifelessly on a medical examination table deep inside the Pit. Scarlett studied the scans of the soldier's body and noticed something strange. She leaned in for a closer look.

"These guys weren't like any soldiers I've ever faced," Duke said. "They didn't even try to evade fire; they just advanced."

Scarlett pointed to a small object on the Neo Viper's scan. "Nanomites," she told the rest of the team. "They'll do whatever they're programmed to do, and they can be programmed to do almost anything."

"Like what?" Ripcord asked.

"Mind control?" Duke asked, thinking that might explain the Neo Vipers' behavior during the battle.

"I don't see why not," Scarlett answered.

"We need to find out who's holding their leash," Duke growled.

Heavy Duty narrowed his eyes, deep in thought. "Their weaponry, financing, intel," he said. "These are pros. Limits the possibilities."

Ripcord had a sudden thought. "The weapons case!" he shouted at the top of his lungs. The others stopped and looked at him like he'd gone nuts, but he knew what he was talking about. "Remember McCullen had us open the case for him?" Ripcord asked. "I'll bet that code he gave us reactivated the tracking beacon or something."

Scarlett considered Ripcord's theory. She hated to admit it, but it made sense. "So McCullen uses NATO to fund his research and then steal it back," she conjectured. The more she thought about it, the more likely it seemed.

Duke looked over at his best friend, obviously impressed. "Who says you're not a thinker?" he asked jokingly.

Just then Breaker came rushing up to them.

"I found her," he announced triumphantly.

Everyone followed Breaker back into the Pit's control room. As soon as they entered, they saw a wedding photo on the monitor in front of them. It was Ana and DeCobray. Duke stared at the photo intensely before confirming that it was definitely the same woman he used to know.

"Her name is Ana DeCobray now," Breaker told them.

"The Baroness, if you're feeling formal."

"Who is he?" Duke asked, pointing to the man in the photo.

"Baron DeCobray is a big shot French scientist," Breaker said. "He runs a lab in Paris."

He punched a few keys on the computer and brought up an image of the Baron working in his lab. Scarlett gazed at the huge machine in the photograph. Breaker informed them that the machine was a particle accelerator, and Scarlett grew concerned.

"They're going to use him to weaponize the warheads," she said.

Duke agreed. "That's definitely where she's going."

"Then so are we," Heavy Duty said.

In a matter of minutes the team had assembled onboard the Howler. The Pit's launch doors opened, and the aircraft took off, streaking at top speed over the desert. The agents stayed silent and focused on the mission at hand—all but Duke, who couldn't keep his mind from thinking about a mission he was on four years ago. . . .

★ ★ ★

It was Ana's brother, Rex's, first mission, and Duke had been in command. He led Rex and Ripcord down a bullet-ridden alley toward their strike target. They took cover just before they reached the building and waited for the rest of the team to give them the all-clear signal to let them know it was safe to enter the building.

Duke remembered asking Rex if he was good to go. He also remembered how terrified Rex was when he nodded. Rex had four minutes to enter the building and find the scientific research they were sent to secure.

"If you don't find it in four minutes, get out of there," Duke warned him. "It won't be standing in five. I already called for the air strike."

Ripcord and Duke provided cover fire as Rex ran into the building. They held off the enemy and kept an eye on their watches. Not even three minutes had passed when Duke heard the sound of jets roaring overhead.

"No, no, no!" he shouted, and took off toward the building. He made it halfway before the bombs dropped out of the sky and flattened the target. There was nothing he could do. Ripcord pulled him onto the waiting helicopter. There didn't seem to be a way that Rex could have survived.

★ ★ ★

As the Howler continued to race toward Paris, Duke wondered how different things would have turned out if those jets hadn't arrived two minutes early. It was Rex's death that drove Ana away from him and most likely to her life of evil. And no matter how hard he tried, Duke couldn't shake the feeling that he was somewhat responsible for this deadly outcome.

ch.13

A black SUV assault truck raced past the Eiffel Tower on its way to the Baron's laboratory. It pulled right up to the entrance, and two shocked security guards looked up to see Ana and Storm Shadow striding in. With a flick of his wrist, Storm Shadow landed a throwing star into each guard, taking them both out. Two Neo Vipers moved in and took the guards' places as Ana led Storm Shadow into the main research chamber.

A giant particle accelerator took up the entire room. Lab technicians swarmed all around it, taking readings and making adjustments. Ana spotted her husband sitting at the control station. She gave the weapons case to Storm Shadow and told him to hang back as she approached the Baron.

No one was more surprised than he to see her in the lab.

"Ana . . . ?" he asked, trying to figure out why on earth she'd shown up.

Ana stayed calm and told her husband that she needed him to do something for her. "I don't have much time," she informed him. She signaled for Storm Shadow to bring the weapons case over to them.

Storm Shadow set the case down and opened it. DeCobray stared at the four warheads, bewildered. "I don't understand," he said. "What are these things? What's going on?"

"They're warheads, dear. And I need you to weaponize them for me," she said, playfully smiling at DeCobray. But her expression changed instantly as she looked around the room. "Do it, or we'll kill *everyone* in here," she threatened.

DeCobray froze with shock; Storm Shadow began losing his patience. He grabbed the pistol from his belt and shot the nearest lab technician.

The terrified workers screamed and ducked for cover. DeCobray fought through his own fear, aware that Ana meant business. He tried to calm his employees. Then he tried to explain to Ana that his lab wasn't set up for the kind of work she wanted him to perform. "We don't have the protocols for weaponizing."

The Baroness flashed a look to let him know she

was annoyed. "The protocols are in the case," she said, sneering. DeCobray took a deep breath, but didn't make any move to start the process. Ana leaned closer to him. "I told you, I don't have much time," she hissed.

Not wanting to see anyone else get hurt, DeCobray reluctantly took the case. He directed his workers to start up the particle accelerator as he entered the protocols into the computer. The machine came to life, and the room filled with a loud hum.

Inside the machine, the four warheads began to spin in a vacuum chamber. Then, as the power grew stronger, they rose and spun around in the air. They spun faster and faster as the accelerator continued to bombard them with atoms. Finally, a loud boom rang out across the room. The warheads slowly stopped spinning and sank back down.

DeCobray keyed another command and the chamber opened. Very carefully, he removed the warheads and returned them to the case. Storm Shadow locked the case and picked it up. "Careful," DeCobray warned him. "They're live."

"Thank you," Ana said, wrapping her arms around him.

DeCobray shook his head. "So this is the face of evil," he said. As soon as the words came out of his mouth, he started gasping for air. His eyes suddenly widened as he glanced down to see Storm Shadow's blade sticking through him.

Ana watched and wished it hadn't ended that way. But her mission was of the highest importance, and sometimes there was a high price to be paid in order to accomplish it.

★ ★ ★

A few blocks away Heavy Duty steered one of the G.I. JOE unit's Brawler attack vehicles through the crowded streets in hot pursuit of the enemy. In the back of the Brawler, Scarlett helped Duke and Ripcord get into their Accelerator Suits, so they could storm the lab as soon as they got there.

Heavy Duty glanced at Duke and Ripcord in the rearview mirror. He still wasn't positive they'd been trained enough, but there was nothing he could do at that point. The unit needed every man they had. "You two stick close to Scarlett and Snake Eyes. Do what they do," he instructed them. "Me and Breaker will stay in the Brawler and watch your backs."

"Yes, Dad!" Ripcord teased. Then he finally noticed that Snake Eyes wasn't suiting up. "What about you? Don't you get one of these?" he asked, glancing at the high-tech armor he was strapped into.

Snake Eyes didn't break his vow of silence, but he didn't need to. One look let Ripcord know it was a silly question. A ninja master didn't need any technology.

"There it is," Heavy Duty announced.

The Brawler cut across traffic and headed straight

for the lab. They got there just in time to see Ana and Storm Shadow climbing back into their truck. Hearing the Brawler approach, Ana glanced in their direction and locked eyes with Duke for a split second. Then she quickly ordered the Neo Viper to get behind the wheel and get them out of there.

Snake Eyes was gone in a flash, grabbing onto the back of the SUV as it sped away.

"Move out!" Heavy Duty shouted to the rest of the team, and Duke leaped out of the Brawler. Ripcord went to follow him when Breaker grabbed him.

"Careful," Breaker told him. "They're worth millions of dollars . . . each."

"Millions, got it!" Ripcord said as he jumped out of the vehicle, only to crash facedown on the pavement. "Sorry!" he yelled over his shoulder, and picked himself up. "I guess these suits are harder to use than I thought."

There was no time for Scarlett to strap into her suit if she wanted to join the chase. She leaped from the Brawler and spied a motorcycle parked nearby. She threw on the Accelerator Suit's helmet, hopped on the bike, and zipped away.

Duke and Ripcord charged after the SUV. The speedometers on their suits climbed to forty miles per hour as they jumped over and around moving cars. The armored SUV smashed through any vehicle in its path as it swerved down the street. Duke and Ripcord followed the trail of destruction, with Scarlett roaring after them from behind.

Snake Eyes clung to the back of the enemy's truck and eventually pulled himself onto the roof. The Baroness and Storm Shadow became alert to the sound of his footsteps above their heads. They drew their weapons, leaned out of their windows, and began firing. Snake Eyes was forced to slither down the side of the vehicle to avoid their shots.

For the first time Ana noticed Duke closing in on them. She leaned back inside the truck and hit a few buttons on the built-in computer, and suddenly the SUV's side panels slid open to reveal a set of missiles.

She launched the missiles with the press of a button. They soared at Duke and Ripcord, who used the power of their suits to dive out of the way. The two missiles whipped between them and barely missed. One of the missiles blew a nearby car to pieces and hurled Duke and Ripcord to the ground as Scarlett tore around the corner. Breaker watched the chase from the monitor screens in the Brawler. He saw that the enemy was getting away, and tried to help Ripcord with a shortcut.

"Go through that building in front of you," Breaker told him over the helmet radio.

"There's no door!" Ripcord shouted back.

"Make one!" Breaker ordered.

Duke never hesitated; he charged right at the building, smashed through the walls, and came out onto another street. Ripcord shrugged his shoulders and followed. The two of them charged up their wrist-mounted rockets, ready to fire, but the SUV was nowhere in sight.

Ripcord scratched his head in confusion, just as the truck thundered up behind them at full speed. He dived out of the way just in time, but Duke had no such luck. He spun around and caught the front of the truck. He dug the suit's mechanical feet into the road and attempted to slow the SUV down.

The Neo Viper drove the truck into a busy intersection, trying to crush Duke in the crisscrossing traffic. Duke was able to throw himself onto the hood just as the truck smashed through another car. Instantly, a pulse cannon popped up from the roof and leveled itself right at Duke.

Duke flung himself off the car a split second before the weapon fired. He tumbled onto the pavement as Ripcord raced up behind him and fired his wrist-mounted rockets. Duke fired with him, and their rockets nailed the SUV. The blast knocked out the pulse cannon, but the rest of the truck was protected by armor, and continued to speed away.

Breaker kept watch from the monitors and tracked the enemy through the streets.

"Where are they heading?" Scarlett asked.

Breaker widened the map. He tried to plot the SUV's route. But the longer he looked at the screen, the less the SUV's course made sense. There was no obvious escape route.

Scarlett suggested that maybe they weren't trying to escape at all; maybe they were going to use the warheads right there in Paris. "Give me a breakdown of all possible targets in the area," she told Breaker.

Breaker transferred the map so that Scarlett could see it on her helmet monitor. The two of them watched the SUV move across the screen. Then they suddenly realized that the Eiffel Tower was directly in its path. Scarlett remembered Hawk telling her that the warheads were programmed to devour metal. "The Eiffel Tower has lots of metal," she said, finally uncovering Ana's plan.

Duke and Ripcord rejoined the chase and took the lead. Scarlett radioed them and made it clear that it was up to them to stop the attack.

"Yeah, we're working on it," Duke told her.

"I mean, you guys have to stop them right *now*!" Scarlett warned. "They're going to detonate one of the warheads on the Eiffel Tower."

Ripcord gasped and glanced up, seeing the famous landmark. "Oh, man . . . " He pushed himself to run even faster.

Snake Eyes hadn't given up either. Having managed to squirm his way to the underside of the speeding SUV, he pulled out his pistol and fired. He blew out the front tires with two shots, and the truck spun out of control. The Neo Viper lost hold of the wheel, and the SUV drove directly into the path of an oncoming Metro train.

Snake Eyes saw the train just in time. He let go of the truck and rolled to safety, just as the SUV was launched into the air. Duke and Ripcord saw the truck flip end over end as they charged toward the train. They were moving too fast to stop and were going to crash too.

Duke managed to leap into the air at the last second.

His boots barely scraped the top of the train. Ripcord wasn't so lucky. He covered his face with his hands and plunged headfirst into the side of a train car! Inside, passengers dived out the way as his Accelerator Suit shredded through the metal and propelled him through to the other side of the car. Seconds later he, Duke, and the SUV all crashed to the ground, and sparks and steel flew in every direction.

Scarlett cringed. She had watched it all from the motorcycle. "You guys okay?"

Duke and Ripcord were shaken up, but they weren't hurt.

"What happened to you?" Duke asked his friend.

"I went through the train," Ripcord told him, shaking himself off. "What happened to you?"

"I jumped over it," Duke said with a smile.

Ripcord was shocked. "You can do that?"

"Yeah, you didn't know?" Duke teased as he helped his friend to his feet.

Inside the SUV, the Neo Vipers were dead. Ana and Storm Shadow were injured but alive. Storm Shadow opened the weapons case and loaded a shoulder launcher with one of the warheads. Ana grabbed the kill switch, and slammed the case shut, and they both took off, with Duke and Ripcord on their tails!

ch.15

Storm Shadow and Ana raced across traffic, dodging cars and shocked spectators. They made a beeline for an office building, with Duke and Ripcord closing in on them. They let nothing get in their way, knocking down anyone who crossed their path. Moments later the two villains plowed their way into the lobby as the sun poured in from the towering glass walls on either side.

With the weapons case in one hand and the kill switch in the other, Ana headed for the glass elevator dead ahead. She cleared the people out of her way by raising a machine gun and pointing it directly at them. "Get. Out," she ordered in a calm but deadly tone.

Amid shock and panic, the innocent men and women rushed out of the elevator. Storm Shadow avoided them with catlike skill, grabbed the case of warheads from Ana, and made his way toward a spiral staircase on the other side of the lobby. Ripcord and Duke came crashing into the building just as he reached the stairs. They caught sight of the ninja just in time to see him scale the staircase and watch the elevator begin its slow climb.

"You get the warheads, I'll get the kill switch!" Duke shouted to Ripcord, and the two split up, using their Accelerator Suits to close in on the targets.

Ripcord sped up the spiral staircase and quickly gained on Storm Shadow. Realizing he was outmatched by the mechanical speed of his pursuer, Storm Shadow exited the stairwell on the next floor and darted down the corridor. Holding the missile launcher on his shoulder, he kicked down a door and escaped into a large corner office lined with tall windows.

Ripcord burst in behind him. Through the windows he had a perfect view of the Eiffel Tower standing majestically a few blocks away. Storm Shadow raised the weapon and took aim. "Don't do it!" Ripcord yelled, grasping the terrible destruction Storm Shadow was about to unleash.

Ripcord lunged toward Storm Shadow. An evil grin spread across the ninja's face as he squeezed the trigger, sending the missile crashing through the glass windows just before Ripcord reached him. As the weapon rocketed through the air, Ripcord and Storm Shadow crashed through a thin wall and fell hard to the ground. But the damage had already been done.

From the ground Breaker watched in horror as the missile hit the Eiffel Tower with a deafening roar. The nanomites erupted from the casing and spread over the landmark like hungry insects. In an instant they began devouring the structure. It only took seconds for the massive metal tower to start crumbling toward the ground.

Heavy Duty shook his head in shock. "They're going to eat through the entire city," he said in horrified disbelief.

Scarlett got on the radio with Duke. "Duke, you have to get that kill switch!" she shouted, unable to contain the urgency in her command.

Duke was climbing the support beams alongside the rising elevator. Ana leveled her machine gun and opened fire, blasting through the glass walls of the elevator and sending splinters of glass raining down on the lobby below. But the gunfire wasn't enough to slow down Duke, and he continued after her.

Once she was out of bullets, Ana reached for her pulse pistol. One blast sent out a sonic shock wave powerful enough to send Duke crashing through the wall of a conference room. Ana used the time to race for the roof, where the Typhoon was hovering above the building, ready to carry her to safety.

Duke sprang back to his feet and went after her. He knew if she got on that helicopter, there would be no way to stop the nanomites from destroying the entire city.

Meanwhile, stunned from the impact of crashing through the wall, Ripcord stumbled to his feet, only to see that Storm Shadow had slipped away. The ninja had already made his way to the top of the building. He joined Ana as a drop rope fell from the waiting airship. The two scurried up, with Duke right on their heels.

Determined to stop them, Duke leaped into the air. The hydraulic suit propelled him into the Typhoon just as it began to pull away. In a flash he overpowered the stunned enemy. He knocked the kill switch from Ana's hands, hit the switch, and then destroyed it. Far below the speeding airship, the nanomites dropped like flies.

Ana allowed a clenched smile to creep across her face as she looked at Duke. "Congratulations," she said in a mocking tone. "You just saved Paris."

Before Duke could react, Storm Shadow snuck up behind him with a fully charged Taser. The shock swept through Duke's body, paralyzing him with pain. He was instantly knocked out cold, dropping to the floor of the retreating Typhoon.

ch.16

Ripcord pushed his way through the crowd that had gathered around the wrecked SUV. He took off his helmet, slipped out of the Accelerator Suit, and wiped the sweat from his forehead. Heavy Duty and Breaker were already on the scene, with the Brawler parked close by. Breaker rushed up to the smoking rubble and yanked one of the dead Neo Vipers from the wreckage. He removed the Neo Viper's armored helmet and reached for a special wire plug from his high-tech surveillance suit.

"What are you doing?" Ripcord asked him.

"Plugging into his cerebral cortex," Breaker said, as if it were something he did every day.

"Ah! Cerebral cortex, right," Ripcord said. He rolled his eyes to make it obvious he had no idea what Breaker was talking about. Then he watched as Breaker plunged the needlelike plug into the top of the Neo Viper's head. The disgusting crunching noise made Ripcord flinch and turn his head.

"The brain survives for a couple of minutes after death," Breaker said.

"We can retrieve the electrical impulses of his most recent memories and convert them to images," Scarlett explained.

"Can you find Duke that way?" Ripcord asked.

"Forget Duke." Heavy Duty sneered. He was focused on the mission. "We need to find the rest of those warheads."

The two G.I. JOE agents glared at each other for a moment until Breaker eased the tension. He told them that if his plan worked, they'd be able to find both Duke and the weapons. He made the last few connections and was able to tap into the Neo Viper's memories. They all watched as a series of images sprang onto the portable screen of Breaker's suit.

The G.I. JOE agents saw the SUV racing along the streets as the images moved backward through time. They saw the Neo Viper inside the lab and aboard the Typhoon gunship. The pictures sped in reverse, and suddenly they saw an image of Ana boarding the Typhoon from a snowy airstrip surrounded by snow-covered mountains.

Breaker hurried to download the image just as the Neo Viper's body started to shake. The sudden movement shocked them, and they all backed away.

"He's still alive!" a surprised Heavy Duty said.

"He's not alive," Scarlett assured him.

"You ever seen a dead guy do that?" Heavy Duty asked.

"They activated a self-destruct," Scarlett said, and pointed to a camera on the Neo Viper's suit. She explained that McCullen was probably watching and didn't want them getting any information. The nanomites inside the Neo Viper were triggered to devour the body.

"They're eating him!" Ripcord shouted in horror.

"Hurry, Breaker!" Scarlett said.

The nanomites worked fast. Breaker rapidly scanned through the memory flashes as the Neo Viper's body turned to dust before their eyes. "Nooo!" he shouted as the nanomites finished the job and left him holding an empty suit in his hands.

Ripcord knelt down next to him. "You did the best you could," he said.

"Relax," Breaker told him as a grin spread across his face. "I got it."

"You got it?" Ripcord asked, completely confused. "Well, what was the 'nooo' for?"

"That was for McCullen," Breaker said. As Hawk

always told them, knowing was half the battle, and Breaker didn't want McCullen to know they'd gotten the information in time. It gave them an advantage.

The team headed for the Brawler and prepared their next move. Just as they were about to climb in, a police SWAT team surrounded them with weapons raised. "Put your hands in the air!" the police captain shouted. Seeing no other choice, the agents shrugged and put their hands in the air.

"We don't have time for this," Ripcord whispered under his breath to the others. Scarlett read his mind. She warned him that it was against orders to fight with friendly forces, but Ripcord thought only about Duke and how the enemy was getting farther away every second. He ignored her warning. He raised his gun and sprayed a burst of gunfire over the heads of the police.

The police hit the deck as Ripcord charged forward, crashing through the line of SWAT forces. From atop a nearby building, Snake Eyes watched as a dozen paratroopers grabbed hold of Ripcord and took him to the ground before he could do any more damage. In a matter of minutes all of the G.I. JOE agents were rounded up and taken into police custody.

In the confusion, Snake Eyes was able to sneak away.

ch.17

In Washington, DC, the president of the United States paced inside the Oval Office. One of his staff had just informed him that the G.I. JOE agents were arrested in Paris. The French government was convinced that G.I. JOE was responsible for the attacks.

"Get me the French ambassador," the president ordered. He turned to another staffer and asked if there was any update on the three remaining warheads. The staffer informed him that they still hadn't found them. After what the first warhead did to the Eiffel Tower, it was critical they were found as soon as possible. The president knew he must get those agents out of prison and on the job. They were the only unit qualified, and there was no time to waste.

He glanced up at the television in his office. The news

channels were teeming with images of the attack in Paris. He shook his head, knowing it wasn't going to be easy to convince the French to let the agents go free after all the damage that had been done.

Meanwhile, from their holding cell, the G.I. JOE agents watched the same footage on a television screen. They saw images of Ripcord rushing at the police. "Nice going, Slick!" Heavy Duty growled. As far as Heavy Duty was concerned, it was all Ripcord's fault that they were in this mess. If he hadn't charged at the police like that, this all would have been cleared up by now.

"It's not his fault," Scarlett defended him. "Rip is just . . . emotional."

Then Scarlett smiled at him, and Ripcord forgot about being locked up for a brief moment. But he came crashing back down to reality when he heard a reporter explain that the terrorists responsible for the attack were in police custody. They all stopped and listened in awe.

"They think *we* did this?" Ripcord growled.

"How could they think this?" Breaker said, just as shocked by the news. "I *love* Paris!"

Heavy Duty glared at Ripcord out of the corners of his eyes, then looked back at the television screen. The news channel replayed the footage of Ripcord going berserk. Ripcord squirmed as he watched, suddenly understanding how the government could think it was their fault.

"Well, we can't just sit here," he said. His mind raced as he tried to think up an escape plan. "They have to take us out for questioning," he said. "When they do, I'll jump the lead guard. Heavy, you—"

"What?" Heavy Duty interrupted. "Start an international incident?"

Ripcord knew it wasn't the smartest plan, but at least he was trying. If they didn't hurry up and do something, they'd never see Duke again. Heavy reminded him that the mission was bigger than just his friend, but Ripcord wouldn't accept that.

"What if it was one of you?" he asked Heavy Duty. "What if they had Breaker or Scarlett, what would you do?"

Heavy Duty looked at his two good friends. Suddenly the plan didn't seem so far-fetched after all.

"Hey, look!" Breaker called out, getting everyone's attention. He pointed to his surveillance suit sitting on the desk outside their cell. One of the detectives had accidentally left the monitor turned on and facing their cell. The last image he'd downloaded from the Viper's memory of Ana boarding the Typhoon on the snowy airstrip was up on the monitor. Just because they were in jail, it didn't mean they were helpless. They got right to work trying to figure out the location.

"Looks pretty remote," Scarlett said. "Might be a good place for a base."

"There's a lot of snow, so that narrows it down," Heavy Duty added.

"Look, we can see the sun and Ana's shadow," Breaker pointed out.

Ripcord rolled his eyes and asked what that had to do with anything. Scarlett just smiled. It was simple trigonometry, she explained.

"I must have missed that class," Ripcord joked.

"To find a latitude and longitude, all you need to know is the height of an object, the length of its shadow, and the time and date the image was recorded," she said.

Breaker scratched his head. "I scanned her outside the lab," he said. "She's five foot ten. Her shadow there is twice that." Then he figured out how old the image was based on how much it had decayed in the Neo Viper's memory. Once he had that, he counted on his fingers and mumbled to himself.

Ripcord watched in amazement as Breaker calculated the coordinates.

"Got it," Breaker announced. "It's the polar ice cap!"

"How did you do that?" Ripcord asked with astonishment. Breaker just shrugged.

The agents were about to plan their next move when the door to the holding room opened.

Scarlett spun around and saw Snake Eyes pushing Hawk in a wheelchair. "General!" she shouted with glee.

As soon as Snake Eyes unlocked the cell gate, she ran up and hugged him.

Hawk took a long look at his team and sighed. He told them that they'd made a real mess of things. The president had had to do a lot of convincing to get them out of there. "The French government is allowing you to leave on the condition that none of you ever return," Hawk said. "Other agencies will be handling this from here on."

"WHAT?" both Ripcord and Heavy Duty blurted out.

"G.I. JOE is now considered uncontrollable. We're being shut down," Hawk told them. "We're to report to Washington for debriefing."

Hawk rolled his wheelchair to the door. Ripcord couldn't believe he was just giving up. "That's it?" he shouted. "They've got Duke!"

Hawk stopped his wheelchair and turned back to the team. "I said you were to report to Washington. I didn't say when or which route to take."

"Maybe a northern one," Scarlett suggested, and Hawk smiled. He told them there was a submarine waiting to transport them as soon as they were released. They couldn't wait to get en route to Washington, DC—after a little detour to the North Pole.

ch.18

Hours later the team was aboard an attack submarine as it neared the polar ice caps. Breaker and Scarlett pored over a 3-D map of the area. They tried to guess where McCullen's secret base was, but it was slow going. There was a lot of area to cover, and lots of potential hiding places.

They caught a major break when a small light flashed on the monitor. "That's strange," Breaker commented.

"What is it?" Scarlett asked.

"When they stole the weapons case, I set my computer to scan for the tracker beacon in case it came back on," Breaker explained. "And it just came back on."

"That's my boy!" Ripcord announced with a grin.

The sub's commanding officer set a new course to follow the beacon.

Inside the icy caves of McCullen's base, Duke paid the price for his heroic act. He had swiped the weapons case and had just enough time to activate the beacon before being attacked. Storm Shadow launched a throwing star into his shoulder, and a group of Neo Vipers charged him.

Duke pulled the throwing star from his shoulder and jammed it into the eye slit of the nearest Neo Viper. The other Neo Vipers surrounded him in a flash. They took him to the ground and continued to pound him. Storm Shadow reached for another throwing star and was ready to strike Duke between the eyes when Ana put an end to the fight.

"Enough!" she hissed, and the others obeyed.

Storm Shadow retrieved the weapons case from Duke, unaware of the tracking beacon being switched on. He sneered over the injured Duke. "What was your plan? Run three thousand miles across the ice?"

The Neo Vipers dragged Duke to his feet, and Ana led him through a hidden door in the cave. An elevator was waiting to take them deep in the ocean and into the base. When the doors opened again, McCullen was there to greet them. Storm Shadow snapped open the case and showed McCullen the three remaining warheads. McCullen ran his fingers over them with satisfaction.

"Take them to the drones," he ordered. "I want them ready to launch in one hour."

"It will be done," Storm Shadow assured him.

McCullen waited until Storm Shadow left, then greeted Ana with a kiss. Duke watched them. He tried to hide his anger, but McCullen noticed his reaction. "Does this bother you?" he asked. Duke kept his mouth shut. McCullen stepped closer. "Isn't it funny, with the entire balance of power in the world about to shift, a couple of guys can still have a stare-down over who gets the girl."

Duke waited for McCullen to get as close as he could. Then, without warning, he flung himself forward and smashed his forehead into McCullen's face.

McCullen wiped a small trickle of blood from his nose as Neo Vipers pummeled Duke to the floor. McCullen gestured for the Neo Vipers to hold Duke steady, and then he bent down. "I'm going to make you very unhappy," he said, sneering.

Duke gritted his teeth. "I'm already unhappy."

McCullen ignored him and headed for the door. He motioned for the Neo Vipers to bring Duke and follow him into the control room. Duke struggled and demanded that McCullen tell him what he planned to do with the warheads. "Isn't it clear?" McCullen said. "I'm going to use them."

"Millions of people are going to die if you launch those warheads," Duke said in a calm voice. "What is it you want?" he asked, trying to reason with McCullen.

It was no use. McCullen had already made up his mind. "I want to strike fear into the hearts of every man, woman, and child on the planet," he told Duke. "Then they will turn to the man who wields the most power."

★ ★ ★

Inside the control room, the Doctor made sketches of cobras as McCullen entered with the captured G.I. JOE agent. Behind him a wall of monitors chronicled Storm Shadow's progress. Duke glanced up at them. He saw three large unmanned drone missiles in their launch bays. A look of horror crept over his face as he realized what McCullen was about to do. He glanced over at Ana and hoped he could reach her, but she quietly looked away.

The Doctor rose to greet McCullen, pausing for several moments to stare at Duke. "Meet the genius behind all my nanotechnology," McCullen said, pointing at the Doctor.

"My genius lies only in taking what others created to the logical next steps," the Doctor explained. "All modern gains in science are made through theft."

McCullen laughed and turned to Duke. "You'll have to excuse the Doctor's modesty," he joked.

The Doctor nodded in Duke's direction. "Another recruit?" he asked McCullen.

"Yes," McCullen told him. "A rather unwilling one."

"I'll prepare him for the procedure," the Doctor said as he smiled under his mask.

Leading the way, the Doctor told the Neo Vipers to bring Duke along to the medical laboratory. Duke gave Ana one last pleading look before being shoved along. She felt sorry for him; somewhere, deep inside, she may have even still loved him. But McCullen was watching her carefully. There was nothing she could do to save him, even if she wanted to.

Outside the underwater base, a school of fish swam past the complex. One of the fish broke away from the others and approached the base. If you looked closely, you could see it was no fish at all. The robotic spy had been sent by G.I. JOE to get a closer look at McCullen's lair and snap surveillance of the defenses.

"The picture's coming online now," Breaker said as the camera transmitted back to the submarine. The team gathered around the monitor and saw what the robotic fish was seeing. The huge underwater facility came on-screen. It was more imposing than they had imagined.

"Duke's gotta be in there somewhere," Ripcord said.

"And the warheads," Heavy Duty added.

As the camera swept across the base, Scarlett noticed a

massive cannon. "Wait," she said. "What's that?"

Breaker zoomed in. "Oh, no," he said. "That's an automated turbo pulse cannon!"

Heavy Duty shook his head. "The main force can't attack as long as that cannon's online," he said.

"Then that's our first objective," Scarlett declared.

"How do you figure getting it off-line?" Ripcord asked.

Snake Eyes pointed to a series of cables that ran from the base to the surface.

"They've got an entrance on the ground," Scarlett said with a smile. She turned to the sub's commanding officer and let him know that's where they planned to enter the base.

He adjusted the submarine's controls. "Going up," he said, and the sub climbed to the ocean's surface. It sped toward the ice, like a bullet, and crashed through. Scarlett led Ripcord, Snake Eyes, and Breaker into the sub's launch bays. The four agents climbed aboard two Rock Slides, their special attack snowmobiles.

"GO, JOE!" they shouted as the vehicles took off.

Heavy Duty waited behind with the rest of the assault team. As soon as Scarlett took out the pulse cannon, they planned to attack underwater with the submarine.

The Rock Slides sped over the ice and into the entrance of the cave. They grounded to a halt inside the base's air hangar, and drew their weapons. Breaker scanned the place from top to bottom as Ripcord stared at the supersonic Night Raven jet parked on the landing strip. It was the most impressive jet he'd ever seen! "That McCullen's got some cool gadgets," he said.

Breaker pointed to a wall of ice and told the others the elevator was behind it. Snake Eyes sliced a hole through the wall with his sword and revealed the elevator cables, but no elevator.

"Maybe we could slide down in our survival suits," Breaker suggested.

Scarlett shook her head and told him the water was too cold. "Even with the suits, we'd freeze before we reached the bottom."

As they tried to figure out how to get down into the base, the ground around them suddenly shook like an earthquake. Then a deafening roar filled the air, and the team rushed out of the hangar to find out what was going on. They made it just in time to see the first drone missile as it shot into the sky, heading east.

Before they could react, a second earthquake erupted and another missile launched. It headed to the west as they heard a third one about to rocket up out of the ground. Snake Eyes thought fast. He sprinted to his Rock Slide and zipped off toward the opening of the missile's launch bay. Then he fired the Rock Slide's two heat-seeking rockets at the target.

The rockets struck the drone, and the sky filled with an explosion of burning metal. The drone was completely destroyed, but the other two were already out of weapons' range.

"Somebody has to go up there and shoot those things down," Scarlett said.

"That's me!" Ripcord volunteered enthusiastically. Then his gaze darted back to the Night Raven. He couldn't wait to get that bird up in the air. He climbed into the cockpit and started flipping switches as he checked out the controls.

Scarlett climbed in beside him and watched him put on the flight helmet. "Can you even fly this thing?" she asked, doubtful of Ripcord's flying ability.

He flashed her a confident smile. "I can fly anything," he told her. "You just track those warheads and guide me in."

Scarlett answered by leaning in and giving Ripcord a kiss. He stared at her, shocked and happy, while she wished him good luck. The grin was still plastered on his face as the Night Raven's engines roared to life. Scarlett and the others watched as the sleek jet zoomed across the sky. Before it was even out of sight, they headed for the launch bays, where the missiles had come from, and sneaked in the back door.

When the third missile disappeared from the

monitors, it alarmed the soldiers in the control room. One of them rushed over and searched for a malfunction in the computer. He checked and double-checked before he finally informed McCullen, "We lost one."

"Lost one? What do you mean?" McCullen growled.

"Bird Three is down, sir."

McCullen glared up at the monitors as the cameras played back images of the third drone being destroyed by an oncoming rocket. He slammed his fist down on the table and gritted his teeth. *That* was definitely not supposed to happen!

Storm Shadow stepped up to McCullen's side. "We're under attack," he said, obviously looking forward to the fight.

Ignoring Storm Shadow's apparent joy, McCullen ordered him to alert all the base's defenses. He wanted his Vipers ready when G.I. JOE arrived!

Strapped to the Doctor's operating table, Duke watched as robots buzzed all around him.

The Doctor hovered over Duke, who was struggling against the straps that held him down. "The atomic bomb that was dropped on Hiroshima destroyed seventy percent of the city. Did you know that, Duke?" the Doctor said as he paced the room.

Duke took a long look at the Doctor. For the first time he noticed something familiar about the strange man hidden behind the mask. "Who are you?" he asked.

The Doctor ignored Duke and continued with his speech. He told Duke about a bank vault near the impact site of the atomic bomb. He explained that the vault survived unharmed, along with everything inside. "Of course, the vault *I* took shelter in wasn't that well made," the Doctor announced as he unclipped the breathing tubes and lowered the mask that covered his face.

Duke stared carefully at the Doctor's badly scarred face. "Rex?" he asked in complete shock.

The Doctor confirmed Duke's suspicions. He nodded, then immediately returned the mask and reconnected his breathing tubes. They both drifted into their thoughts and returned to the day four years ago when Rex was left trapped in the collapsed building.

Duke remembered how frantically he had tried to reach Rex on the radio. He had yelled for Rex to get out before it was too late. He didn't understand why Rex had let everyone think he was dead; why he had chosen to be left behind?

"Why didn't you come in?" Duke asked.

"Because," the Doctor answered, "I found out the truth!"

He filled Duke in on the missing details of that fateful mission. After he'd entered the building, he'd made his way to where the laboratory was supposed to be, only to find a vault instead. There was an old scientist inside, along with a computer that contained the information on the research that Rex was sent to collect. But the research had nothing to do with chemical or nuclear weapons, as the army had led Rex to believe. Instead, it was all the information on the first nanotechnology experiments.

They were far beyond anything Rex had ever thought existed.

"The man who created this technology was not our enemy," he told Duke. Rex had talked to the scientist briefly before the explosion and learned everything. "In fact, he was hired by our very own government to create it. Then they sent us to kill him!"

If Duke was surprised, he didn't let it show. He knew the army had sent him on some shady missions in the past, but he understood that it was part of the job. He accepted that the army had good reasons, even if he didn't know what they were. But Rex had always been more idealistic, and Duke imagined how betrayed he must have felt when he found out.

"The scientist didn't survive the blast," the Doctor told him. "But I lived . . . sort of. And I escaped with his research. Now I've perfected it, and you're going to get a firsthand demonstration."

Duke thought back to the Neo Viper who he and his fellow soldiers had examined after the battle in the Pit. Scarlett told him the nanomites were injected into the subject, destroying the brain and making it easy for the soldier to be controlled. It dawned on him that the Doctor planned on doing the same sick experiment on him. He never thought his old friend would turn to this kind of life; then again, he never thought Ana would either.

"Why would you work for McCullen?" Duke asked him.

"He saved my life, for starters." The Doctor tapped the breathing mask, making it clear that the technology came from McCullen's factory. "He also has infinite resources and understands that with science, it's sometimes necessary to destroy in order to attain a goal."

As the robots moved closer, Duke realized that the Doctor had tried this experiment many times. Then he remembered all the nervous glances from Ana. To Duke, it seemed like she'd been struggling with something. He couldn't explain it before, but it made sense at that moment. "You did this to Ana, didn't you?" he accused his former friend.

"I had to!" the Doctor shouted. "Do you have any idea the state she was in? *Me, dead. You, AWOL!* I brought her here and gave her a way to deal with her pain. I made her strong. I gave her a new life, Duke. You abandoned her!"

The Doctor's words stung Duke. He'd always felt guilty about the way he went sort of crazy after Rex died. He knew he'd left Ana when she'd needed him most.

Satisfied that his words had gotten to Duke, the Doctor moved behind the control panel. He entered a series of commands into the computer, and the robots moved in even closer on Duke. Once the nanomites took over, Duke would be under the Doctor's complete control!

ch.21

After descending the narrow missile chambers, Scarlett, Snake Eyes, and Breaker dropped into the scorched launch bay. Directly in front of them was the hallway that led into the main base. The walls, floor, and ceiling of the passage were lined with metal and protected by lasers. "Is there any way around them?" Scarlett asked, and reminded the others that they had to hurry and get the pulse cannon off-line before the sub could attack.

Breaker scanned the hallway. "No," he said. There was only one way into the main section—through the lasers. "Anything larger than a quarter that touches the floor will fry."

Snake Eyes sighed and shook his head. It wasn't going to be any kind of obstacle for him. He stepped forward and dived into the hall, landing on his fingertips. Using all his strength to keep his balance, he walked across the floor on his fingertips. The hum of lasers surrounded him as he made his way through.

Scarlett and Breaker held their breaths until Snake Eyes reached the other side. Relieved, Breaker directed him to the laser's control panel. "What you have to do is rewire . . . ," he started to explain, but Snake Eyes had a different plan. Balancing on one hand, he grabbed his sword with the other and stabbed it into the control panel. "Or you could just do that," Breaker said as the lasers vanished.

Scarlett and Breaker ran ahead and joined Snake Eyes. The three of them headed for the pulse cannon's control room. Two Vipers were at the cannon's controls, firing away at the G.I. JOE submarine. Snake Eyes charged at the Vipers and took them out. With no one at the controls, the cannon powered down. Snake Eyes sent a quick message to Heavy Duty over his wrist-communicator and gave him the all-clear for the assault.

The message popped up on the sub's screen. "Cannon off-line. Have a nice day," Heavy Duty read. Then he smiled and turned to the sub's commanding officer. "Let's get in this fight," he said.

The G.I. JOE submarine peeled around a rocky underwater cliff and came in full view of McCullen's base. Once in position, it fired a series of torpedoes from its tubes. The base's other defense guns managed to blow up most of the torpedoes, but several hit their target.

The whole place was shaking from the explosions as Scarlett and Breaker made their way to the Flight Control Room. They blew open the doors and entered. Inside, the room was guarded by Vipers. Scarlett cut them down, and Breaker took over the computer console.

"I've got a lock on the two warheads," he said. "Target one is Moscow! Target two is Washington!"

Scarlett radioed to Ripcord and gave him the coordinates. The Night Raven soared near the top of Earth's atmosphere, already on the tail of the first target. "I see it, dead ahead!" he told Scarlett.

"You have to knock it down before it re-enters the atmosphere, so the nanomites don't reach the ground," Breaker told him.

Ripcord flicked a switch, but there were no fire controls anywhere to be found. With panic in his voice, he reported the problem back to Breaker and Scarlett.

"It's got to be voice-activated," Scarlett told him. "You have to say the words into your flight helmet."

Ripcord got a lock on the warhead and shouted, "FIRE!" Nothing happened, so he tried again. "Shoot! Blast away!" But the Night Raven's weapons didn't respond, and the warhead continued to streak toward its target.

"Try *teine*," Scarlett suggested. "It's Scottish for 'fire.'"

Ripcord wasn't so sure about that plan, but he gave it

a try. *"Teine,"* he said and still nothing happened. *"Teine! Teine!"* he yelled twice more before telling Scarlett that it wasn't working.

"That's because you're not saying it right!" she yelled. She pronounced the word slowly, and Ripcord repeated it. The jet's lasers fired and blasted the missile out of the sky. Ripcord sighed with relief as he saw a cloud of nanomites float away into space.

"Nice work, Ace!" Breaker shouted. "You just saved Moscow!"

"Just doing my job," Ripcord said, playing it cool. "Now guide me to the other one."

ch.22

Back at the pulse cannon, Snake Eyes stayed put, ready to fight off anyone who tried to switch the defenses back on. He kept his eyes peeled for Neo Vipers, unaware that Storm Shadow had sneaked in behind him.

A sudden rush of air made Snake Eyes spin around. He saw two blades come crashing down and was only able to dodge one of them. The other blade cut his left arm and sent him reeling backward.

With Snake Eyes momentarily out of the way, Storm Shadow powered the pulse cannon back online. Then he spun around and blocked Snake Eyes' blades as they swung for his head.

In an instant the two ninjas resumed the conflict that had started when they were ten years old. Their blades flashed like lightning as they battled fiercely. Storm Shadow drove Snake Eyes away from the cannon, and a Neo Viper slid behind the controls. Locked in combat, Snake Eyes was unable to stop him, and the cannon began blasting again.

A bright blue pulse rippled through the ocean and struck the G.I. JOE submarine! The sub shook as the shot blasted a hole into the ship's side. "The hull's been ruptured!" the sub's commanding officer shouted.

"Everyone to the attack boats!" Heavy Duty ordered.

They rushed to the waiting ships as hatches opened all along the side of the sub. Ten SHARC attack crafts launched, carrying the agents into battle. They were followed by a dozen MANTIS attack ships piloted by Neo Vipers.

The two fleets raced forward on a collision course. "Keep tight, everybody," Heavy Duty radioed out. Then he fired a torpedo, destroying one of the MANTIS crafts.

The other MANTIS ships opened fire as the pulse cannon let off another volley. It hit the abandoned sub, which exploded in a fireball hurling toward the base!

Another blast destroyed one of the SHARC crafts. Heavy Duty returned fire. He took out another MANTIS, but the odds were stacked against them as long as the pulse cannon was still firing.

"That cannon's going to kill us all," the sub's commanding officer said.

Heavy Duty was still counting on one thing: Snake Eyes.

ch.23

Duke winced in pain as a robot made a small incision behind his right ear. Then a large needle moved in, ready to inject the nanomites into his body. Duke braced himself, but before the needle hit his head, someone at the control panel flicked a switch.

The robots reversed and moved away from Duke. He looked over and saw the Doctor was knocked out on the floor. Ana had taken over the controls. She rushed over and untied Duke. "I don't have much time," she told him, and tried to hurry him along, but he didn't care. He reached up for her, and they kissed.

Duke's hand felt something behind Ana's ear, and he turned her head. Just as he'd thought, there was an incision scar. As he was about to tell her what was going on, her body suddenly went weak and fell limp into his arms.

He looked over his shoulder and saw the Doctor holding the handheld computer that controlled all the soldiers. McCullen was with him, along with two Neo Vipers with rifles aimed at Duke.

"Is she still alive?" McCullen asked the Doctor.

"For now," he responded.

"I thought we had complete control!" McCullen roared. "You said this couldn't happen."

"I didn't think it could," the Doctor explained. "I've never seen anyone defeat the programming before."

As they talked, Duke grabbed one of the pulse pistols from Ana's holster. He leveled two quick shots, killing the Neo Vipers before he turned the weapon on McCullen.

The Doctor held up the handheld computer and warned Duke not to fire. He showed Duke that his finger was on the terminate button. "If I press this, Ana dies. Your choice, Duke."

"Put it down, Rex," Duke pleaded. "This is your sister!"

McCullen watched the standoff silently as he carefully sneaked up on Duke. Duke stayed focused on the Doctor and didn't notice McCullen's hand as it drew a steel hose from his sleeve.

"Did you think she loved you?" McCullen said, sneering, now only a few feet away from Duke.

Duke whipped around in surprise. "Stay back!" Duke shouted.

"Did you imagine a life with her?" McCullen asked as he moved closer.

"I said, stay back!"

"Don't you know you've lost, Duke?" the Doctor chimed in.

"All I know is that neither of you deserves her!" Duke yelled just as McCullen lifted the steel hose and aimed it at Duke. A burst of flame shot out, and Duke instinctively fired Ana's pulse pistol at it. The intense blast of air from the pistol caught the flames and blew them back at McCullen!

McCullen screamed as his face caught on fire. The Doctor dropped the device in his hands and pulled McCullen away in retreat. Duke fired after them as he made his way across the room. The Doctor avoided his shots and got away with McCullen.

Duke wanted to chase after them, but he had other concerns. He picked up the handheld device and safely switched off the nanomites that controlled Ana.

Back at the White House, the president watched the progress of G.I. JOE's assault from the Oval Office. And though the first two warheads were destroyed, there was still one headed straight for Washington, DC.

"How soon will it strike the city?" he asked one of his men.

"Seventeen minutes, sir."

Too close to take any chances, the Secret Service rushed the president and his staff into a fortified bunker. "This will be a disaster, the likes of which we have never seen," the president said gravely once they were inside.

As soon as he finished talking, a Neo Viper, disguised as one of the Secret Service agents, drew a silenced pistol and killed the others before they could react.

The president stared in horror as the Neo Viper turned the pistol on him. He led the president to a bookcase inside the bunker. The bookcase moved along the wall and revealed a hidden room. The president watched a figure as it moved out of the shadows.

"Oh, no," the president whispered in shock as a man who looked identical to him stepped closer.

★ ★ ★

Thousands of miles away, Snake Eyes was also in a tight spot. Storm Shadow drove him farther and farther away from the pulse cannon. With the Viper left in control, the SHARC crafts were pinned under heavy fire.

Several Neo Vipers joined Storm Shadow. They distracted Snake Eyes just enough to keep him from getting the jump on his old enemy. Storm Shadow took advantage of the situation and lunged at Snake Eyes. The two warriors collided and tumbled down a deep shaft where the icy waters waited for them hundreds of feet below. Two Neo Vipers got caught in the collision and went along for the ride. Both Storm Shadow and Snake Eyes crashed down on a narrow gangway that cut across the pit and pulled themselves to safety. The Neo Vipers weren't so lucky. They sank into the ocean below and froze instantly.

As Snake Eyes and Storm Shadow sprang back to their feet, the shaft filled with a blaring noise. The two ninjas glanced around and noticed the circuits all up and down the walls. The noise grew even louder as the circuits charged up to power the cannon. A moment later a laser shot out and connected each of the circuits in a deadly net. One of them caught Storm Shadow's shoulder and burned him. Snake Eyes saw this and ducked just as another laser fired beside his head.

Storm Shadow recovered quickly and slashed Snake Eyes across the chest. Snake Eyes stumbled, and Storm Shadow prepared to finish him off. He raised his blade, ready to level it into Snake Eyes just as the cannon fired and the laser net vanished. It only took a moment for another net to weave across. Storm Shadow had to twist his body away for a split second. It gave Snake Eyes a chance to get back on his feet and lift his blade into one of the shimmering beams of laser light. The laser was sent screaming back at Storm Shadow, who raised his sword just in time to deflect it.

After the cannon released its pulse charge, the laser net disappeared again. The two men glared at each other, prepared for their final duel. They'd been facing off since they were kids, and neither was ever able to defeat the other. There was finally going to be a winner. It was the moment Snake Eyes had waited for since the day he remembered Storm Shadow killing their master in a fit of rage and running away from the temple.

"You took your vow of silence to avenge our master,"

Storm Shadow mocked Snake Eyes. "But now you will die without a word."

He charged at Snake Eyes just as the loud hum started up again. The noise briefly distracted Storm Shadow, and Snake Eyes took advantage of the moment. He caught his enemy in a leg lock and used all his strength to lift Storm Shadow into the air just as the lasers came back on. He held him there and watched as one of them sliced across Storm Shadow's neck!

Storm Shadow screamed. He was left clutching at his throat. Snake Eyes released him, and Storm Shadow stumbled backward in pain. Losing his balance, he tumbled over the edge and into the icy water below.

Snake Eyes peered over the edge to see if Storm Shadow would resurface. Once he saw that his sworn enemy was gone and that he'd avenged the death of his master, Snake Eyes took out the circuits on the wall. The walls vibrated, and he quickly climbed out of the shaft as it erupted in a violent explosion.

In one of the SHARC attack crafts, Heavy Duty hollered with excitement when he saw the cannon go off-line. "The pulse cannon is down!" he announced to the rest of the fleet. They gunned their engines and were quickly able to turn the tide of the battle. The MANTIS vehicles were destroyed in a flash of fire as they squared around and headed directly for the base.

ch.25

Up in the skies, Ripcord spotted the second warhead in front of him. "Second drone in my sights," he told Breaker as the missile rocketed downward.

Breaker watched the drone's path on the monitors in the Flight Control Room. "Hurry, Rip," he said frantically. "You've only got thirty seconds before it enters the lower atmosphere."

Ripcord punched the Night Raven's thrusters and targeted the missile. *"Teine!"* he screamed out, but nothing happened.

Scarlett heard him over the com-system. *"Teine!"* she corrected him.

Ripcord took a breath to steady his nerves. The fuel light on the Night Raven's control board beeped, but he did his best to ignore it. He focused on the warhead as it began to drop into the lower atmosphere. He cleared his throat and gave the command a second try: *"Teine!"*

On the monitor, Breaker watched the jet's missile track off course. It sailed harmlessly past the warhead and into space. "You missed!" he shouted. "The warhead has entered the lower atmosphere!"

Ripcord realized this as he entered the lower atmosphere, too. He saw Washington, DC, spread out far below, and he began to sweat. He dipped the jet's nose down and sped after the drone. He wanted to move in close to make sure there was no chance he'd miss again.

Scarlett and Breaker saw the aircraft closing in on the missile. "You're too close," Breaker warned. "Rip, back up!"

"Actually, I think I'm just about close enough," Ripcord told them before he gave the order to fire. *"Teine!"*

The jet's lasers struck the drone from point blank range, and it exploded! Ripcord flew through the flames, and the cloud of nanomites latched onto the Night Raven's wings. They swiftly ate through the metal, and Ripcord struggled with the controls. The fuel light flashed faster, too, and Ripcord had to act rapidly. He pointed the Night Raven upward at top speed as it started to break apart all around him.

"He's taking the nanomites back up into the

atmosphere," Breaker said when he saw the image of the jet climbing on the monitor.

Scarlett watched in horror and begged Ripcord to eject himself.

Ripcord attached his flight helmet's breathing mask and turned the plane upside down so that he could see the ground miles below. Scarlett told him the Scottish word for "eject," and Ripcord repeated it. *"Cur magh!"* he yelled, and the cockpit canopy exploded, shooting Ripcord back down to earth.

As he fell through the sky, Ripcord saw the nanomites devour the rest of the Night Raven. Then, with a smile, he watched them float away into space.

"Ripcord?" Scarlett's voice screamed into his helmet. "Talk to me! Are you okay?"

Ripcord smiled even wider as his parachute opened. "Yeah," he said, thrilled that she was so concerned about him. "Did it work?" he asked.

"Yes! Yes, it worked," a relieved Scarlett told him.

"Good," Ripcord said as he looked down and saw the White House below him. "Because I think I'm about to get arrested again," he added, spotting dozens of Secret Service agents waiting to take him in as soon as he touched down.

ch.26

As the G.I. JOE attack crafts continued to fire at the base, explosions flared up all around Breaker and Scarlett. The Flight Control Room took a direct hit, and the whole place shook. Another blast sent water flowing in and caused the monitors to short out.

"The power subsystems are going critical," Breaker said.

"Let's get out of here!" Scarlett yelled. She grabbed Breaker by his surveillance suit and hauled him out of the room.

They raced through the burning halls toward the elevator that would take them back to the surface. When they arrived, they were shocked to find a badly wounded Snake Eyes already waiting for them.

Scarlett rushed ahead and gently hugged Snake Eyes. He grimaced in pain. Then they turned to see Duke running toward them, carrying Ana in his arms. Another explosion made them all dash into the elevator. With the push of a button, it launched them to safety.

On another level of the base, the Doctor helped the horribly burned McCullen into the Trident submarine. The pilots hurried to the controls and guided the sub out of the docking bay as explosions rang out all around.

In his SHARC, Heavy Duty noticed the Trident escaping and steered his craft on an intercept course. "We got a runner!" he shouted, just as the entire base exploded behind him.

A massive chunk of ice plummeted down and cut off Heavy Duty's pursuit. He watched as the submarine escaped; he had no choice but to let it go. Their commanding officer quickly informed him that all the other targets had been destroyed. Satisfied that the mission was a success, Heavy Duty ordered the other agents to the surface as the Trident disappeared into the depths of the ocean.

Onboard the escaping sub, the Doctor injected McCullen with nanomites. The tiny robots worked furiously and created a form-fitting mask over Destro's scorched face.

After the pain subsided, McCullen dared to face his reflection in the mirror. Seeing the metallic mask, he broke down and fell to the floor in horror. He slowly recovered and looked up at the Doctor. "I guess I should thank you," he said.

The Doctor fiddled with a small device in his hands, and McCullen realized that he was now at the Doctor's mercy. "From now on," the Doctor said, sneering, "I'll be on a first name basis with you, *Destro*. And I want you to call me *commander.*"

McCullen's silver face went blank, powerless to resist.

"Yes, Commander."

On the surface of the polar ice caps, G.I. JOE celebrated its victory. Little did they know, the battle had unleashed a more dangerous enemy than McCullen had ever hoped to become!

ch.27

In the days after the battle, Ana was under constant medical supervision inside G.I. JOE's maximum-security prison. On one of his many visits, Duke watched her through a two-way mirror. The medic had run countless tests trying to figure out a way to free Ana completely from the nanomites in her body. So far he'd had no luck. "I've never seen encoding like this," he told Duke. "Whoever programmed those things sure didn't want them shut off."

"There's nothing you can do?" Duke asked.

"Only the man who put them in there can take them out," the medic explained.

Duke considered this carefully. "Then I know what I've gotta do," he said. Rex was responsible for this, and

Duke was willing to do whatever it took to track him down. For Ana's sake, he had to.

The medic patted Duke on the shoulder as he left. Alone, Duke waited for two prison guards to take Ana from the medical examination room. He watched through the mirror as they shackled her hands and feet before bringing her into the hall where he waited. As they led her back to her cell, he walked alongside her.

"You're gonna be seeing a lot me around here," he promised her.

"It's no use," she said, letting her black hair cover her face.

"I'm not going away, Ana." Duke needed her to know that he wasn't going to leave her this time, not like before. "We're going to beat this."

"You can't save me, Duke. No one can," Ana told him. "Not after all I've done."

"It wasn't *you* who did those things," Duke reminded her.

"It was more of me than you want to believe," Ana confessed. Then she turned away and mumbled to herself, "And when it happens . . . it feels good."

When they reached her cell, Duke promised Ana again that he wasn't going to give up on her. For a moment she looked at him with her eyes full of hope. But then something changed inside her, and a sinister grin crept across her face.

"You know, this has only just begun," she said, her voice almost robotic as she reached up and touched the scar behind Duke's ear. Duke flinched, and the guards backed her into her cell. Duke watched in silence as the bars slammed shut between them. His face was torn with pain as he realized Ana would never be completely out of Rex's clutches as long as those things were inside her.

He slowly made his way back to the Pit's landing platform, where General Hawk was waiting to give new orders. Heavy Duty, Breaker, Ripcord, and Scarlett were already standing beside the Howler when Duke approached.

"With G.I. JOE reinstated, Heavy Duty here recommended that you boys stick around," Hawk told Duke and Ripcord.

Duke smiled. "That's what we're planning, sir."

The others surrounded them and gave them welcoming pats on their backs. But there wasn't a lot of time for congratulations with McCullen and the Doctor still on the loose. General Hawk was eager to get back to work and hand his team their new top secret orders.

The agents climbed aboard the Howler, ready for action.

"Yo, JOE!" they cheered.

The hatch slammed shut, and the Howler's engines

fired up. In no time they were thundering across the sky, ready to save the world again.

But, little did any of them know, the enemy was closer than they thought.

McCullen's plan hadn't been a total disaster. In fact, the Commander saw it as a complete success, because the most important part had gone perfectly. Zartan's physical disguise fooled everyone. Certainly the loss of the warheads and the underwater base was substantial, but it was an acceptable price to pay for control of the free world. Even the first lady and the White House staff members couldn't tell that the one sitting behind the president's desk in the Oval Office wasn't actually the president.

There was no telling what kind of damage they would be able to do with Zartan acting as president! One thing was certain, however: G.I. JOE would have to work twice as hard if they hoped to win the next battle!